A TIME TO RUN
STUART AND SAM

Library and Archives Canada Cataloguing in Publication
Schultz Nicholson, Lorna, author
A time to run : Stuart and Sam / Lorna Schultz Nicholson.
(One-2-one)
Issued in print and electronic formats.
ISBN 978-1-988347-09-7 (softcover).--ISBN 978-1-988347-10-3 (PDF)
I. Title. II. Title: Stuart and Sam. III. Series: Schultz Nicholson, Lorna.
One-to-one.
PS8637.C58T56 2018   jC813'.6   C2018-900341-3
C2018-900342-1

Design concept by Tanya Montini
Interior and cover design by CommTech Unlimited
Printed in Canada by Webcom

A TIME TO RUN
STUART AND SAM

A ONE-2-ONE BOOK

Lorna Schultz Nicholson

CLOCKWISE
PRESS

AUTHOR'S NOTE

The Best Buddies is a real program that operates in schools, including colleges, all over the world. Students with intellectual disabilities, including people with autism, pair up with volunteer peer "Buddies." They meet together, one-to-one, at least once a month to engage in fun, social interactions. They also participate in group activities. That said, this is a work of fiction. Stuart and Sam are fictional characters and I made them up. I also made up where they live, their high school, their families and all their situations. Yes, I did a tremendous amount of research so I could write this novel but, in the end, it is a work of fiction. This fiction is pleasure reading. So, please, enjoy!

This book is dedicated to the Rossi clan.

- L.S.N

CHAPTER ONE
STUART

My body vibrated. The cheerleaders bounced up and down on their toes and waved their blue-and-white pom-poms. The noise in the gym sounded like a booming bass drum and I *liked it*. I watched the cheerleaders as they dropped their pom-poms and ran to do cartwheels and flips. My job was to stay quiet on the bench, and give out towels and water bottles.

More cartwheels. More cheering. More buzzing. The gym was like a video game on high speed, so many colours, all moving and spinning and changing. Our school, Sir Winston Churchill, was playing in the city finals against Woodland School. HUGE basketball game. My Best Buddy, Sam, was the team captain and one of the best scorers because he could run fast. I needed to run or do something. Right now!

One of the cheerleaders did a back flip. I jumped up off the bench, stuck my hands up, ran forward, and did a front flip too, something I'd learned to do on the trampoline ages ago.

When I landed, I felt a tug on my shirt. "Don't do that," whispered Cassandra, the team trainer. She tried to pull me back to the bench.

But I wanted to do another flip. I stuck my arms in the air.

"You're not a cheerleader," she said, still whispering, and tugged on my shirt. "You're the team manager. Sit on the bench."

"I'm not the team manager," I said. But I liked being called the team manager better than the water boy so I sat down. Water boy sounded totally lame. Team manager sounded cool.

Cassandra leaned over. "I like the stars you put on the water bottles."

I looked down at the green water bottles I had filled up. At first, I had just put a star on Sam's but then he had told me to put a star on every bottle. He said a team is a team. Before every practice, we pumped our fists together and he said *we* were a team, meaning him and me, and I liked that because it meant I had a friend. Kids don't really like me. My mom says that's okay, that not everyone will like me. I guess I don't care that no one likes me, but then sometimes I do care. A lot.

The cheerleaders kept jumping and cheering and they got the crowd going. The noise made my body jittery. Metal music does the same thing. Now, at home, I have to sneak into Declan's room if I want to listen to anything heavy. Declan is my biological brother. The noise in the gym got louder and louder and I stood and yelled along with everyone.

Go Greyhounds, go!

Go Greyhounds, go!

There was no way I could be banned from the gym. Well, okay, I could. But not for cheering for the basketball team. I could be as loud as I bloody well wanted. The cheerleaders danced and flipped around and then...the real song came on. "We Are the Champions" by Queen. During playoffs, they play this song when the basketball team runs onto the court just before the start of the game.

The cheerleaders moved to the side and I watched as the other team came out first and their fans cheered. A yellow bus full of kids from the other school had come to watch the game. I booed. Cassandra pulled on my shirt and told me to be quiet. I booed again.

Then our team came flying out and the crowd revved up totally. I felt fueled, like I'd just had a Red Bull. This time Cassandra didn't say anything to me.

Both teams warmed up by taking shots on net. Basketballs bounced on the wooden floor. Then the buzzer blew and all the players came over to the bench and that's when I started handing them each a water bottle, the one with their name on it. Now, only the referees were on the court. They stood in front of the table where the scorekeepers sat. After getting their bottles, the players gave me a high-five, but only Sam gave me a high-five *and* a wink.

An announcer came on and we had to stand to listen to "O Canada." *Booooring*. I wished it was rap instead.

Once the song was over the announcer spoke again and said the names of the players who would start the game. When Sam's name was announced I clapped so hard my hands hurt. He ran onto the court and took his place in the middle circle. He told me that he didn't take the jump ball because he wasn't the tallest, but Cecil did because he was almost as tall as a door and skinny like a string. His black dreadlocks were so cool.

The starting lineup crouched around the centre circle. The gym went silent. The whistle blew, the ref threw the ball, and the players ran, and I could hear feet on the floor and a basketball bouncing. Sam was the one bouncing the ball and running down the court with it. Coach Nelson liked him taking the ball down the court—called him the *guard man*—because he was the best passer on the team. He was good at setting up the play.

Sam slowed down and they set up. The ball went from player to player like a video clip. *Boom. Boom. Boom.* My eyes followed the ball, just like when I played video games. Back and forth. Back and forth. I watched the ball. Sometimes Sam and I played 21 together. He told me to always watch the ball. Then Sam got the ball, jumped, and swooshed it through the net. I stood, cupped my hands around my mouth, and screamed!

The crowd screamed and my heart pounded against my skin.

The players ran down the court again, this time the other way. But then Sam just grabbed the ball right out of the air when the other team tried to pass it across the court. Suddenly he was heading to the other team's basket—alone!

Sneakers screeched on the floor. All the players turned to run back the other way, trying to catch him. I stood up.

"Go, Sam!"

Sam booked it to the net. His legs stretched as he took his two steps in his lay-up and jumped way up into the air. The basketball hit the backboard and went into the net.

"Yeah, Sam!" I yelled.

He landed but instead of running, he fell. Like, *crumpled down*. Then he just lay on the ground and didn't move.

"Sam!" I yelled. *Why didn't he get up?* I jumped on the bench, cupped my hands around my mouth, and yelled, "Get up!"

"Oh, my God," said Cassandra.

He didn't get up. He didn't. He just lay there on the gym floor. The ref blew the whistle. Players leaned over him. Cassandra sped onto the court, running like I'd never seen her run before. I had to go to him too. Help him up. I heard Cassandra tell everyone to back away. But I wanted to see Sam. I started to run over to him when someone grabbed my shirt.

"Don't get in the way," said Angelo, a player from the team. I didn't like Angelo much.

"Let me go," I said.

"The coaches and trainers need space," he said.

"Get your hands off of me!"

"Why don't you ever listen?" He shook his head at me but still hung on to my shirt.

"I don't have to listen to you."

"Dude, come on. You can't go over there."

"Just watch me," I said.

I squirmed and squirmed, trying to get away from Angelo, but he was too strong. "Someone help me," he called out. "The kid's gonna run, again."

No way. I didn't want two against one. Two against one sucked big time. And three was worse. I yanked my arm away from Angelo, but because I pulled so hard, I stumbled and fell. I crawled along the floor and hopped up before he could catch me. And I ran toward Sam.

"Sam!" I screamed.

Cassandra had her fingers on Sam's neck. Then she just started pumping up and down on his chest. "Get the AED," she yelled. "Now!"

What was an AED? Whatever it was, it didn't sound good. My whole body started shaking and I screamed again for Sam to *get up*. Cassandra was hurting Sam, pounding on him like that.

People all around me were moving fast.

"Stuart, stay back," said Coach Nelson.

"Sam!" I yelled as loudly as I could, so he could hear me. But he wasn't moving.

I felt arms around me and by the smell of soap and the dark colour on the arms I knew it was my dad. My entire family had come to watch the game. He's not my biological dad but my adopted dad, and it's obvious he's not my real dad because I'm white and he's black. Same with my mom. He held me close, like his arms were bungee cords that had been stretched tight.

"Stay with me," he whispered in my ear. "And stop screaming. It's not helping." I wrestled against his arms, trying to free myself, but he held on. My dad has huge biceps because he used to be a CFL football player.

The trainer just ripped Sam's shirt off and put something right on his skin. The machine talked. And it said, "*Shock.*"

"They're going to hurt him!"

"*Shhh*," whispered my dad in my ear.

Sam's body jumped but then nothing.

"Come on, Sam," said Cassandra.

"Breathe, breathe," said Coach Nelson.

Again, the machine said, "*Shock.*"

"Come on, Sammy," my father whispered.

This time when Sam's body jumped, he made a noise.

"He groaned," said Coach Nelson.

I tried to get away from my dad again. What they were doing to Sam seemed wrong.

My dad tightened his arms around me, squeezing me. A man and a woman dressed in uniforms rushed into the gym with a stretcher. It was like the world was moving on fast forward. The people with the stretcher put Sam on it and wheeled him out, running beside him. I wanted to run with them, but my dad still held onto me.

"Why won't you let go of me?"

"Stuart, no one can do their job if you're in the way. You'll only make it worse for Sam. Is that what you want? To hurt him more?"

"NO!"

"Then let the paramedics do their job."

I wriggled some more. But my dad was still the one person who could hold me back. One day I might be big enough to get away from him, but right now I was the smallest kid my age. Finally, I gave up.

"Where are they taking him?" I whispered.

"To the hospital," said my father.

"The hospital?"

I felt like a slashed car tire losing air. My body felt floppy. I leaned into my dad. He hugged me and kissed the top of my head.

"Is he…gonna be okay?"

"I hope so," he said.

CHAPTER TWO
SAM

The ball flew across the court, a pass by the other team, and I knew it was within my reach. Two quick steps and I would have it, with a perfect line to the net. I bolted forward, jumped, and nabbed the ball mid-air, feeling its rough ridges on the tips of my fingers. *Hang onto it. Hang on.* One dribble for control and I took off down the court, bouncing the ball in front of me, controlled bounces—no way I was letting this ball get away from me. Behind me, shoes squealed on the floor. I knew that nine players had abruptly turned to give chase. Five from the other team were out to stop me.

Keep going. Don't stop. Legs moving. Run.

Now I was alone, open, and heading toward the basket, feet still behind me, trying to catch me. I had to push harder, move faster. I ignored the pounding in my head, the sudden searing in my chest, only wanting the ball in the hoop. Two points on the scoreboard. Close, I lengthened my stride, took my two steps for my lay-up, steps I'd practised since I was a kid. My body lifted and…shooting pain.

Stabbing me.

Everything blurred in front of me. My chest burned, like I'd been branded with a hot iron. My head pounded, like it was being hacked in two.

Where was the basket? The backboard?

It was as if a rubber band was pinching my heart, tighter, tighter, tighter. The elastic stretching, wanting to snap. I grabbed my chest. I couldn't breathe. No air. My lungs burned.

More blurriness. Haze. Fog. I couldn't see.

Anything.

But black. Black. Black.

Where was I? I tried to peel open my eyes, but the under side of my eyelids felt like sand had been shoved in there, making them scratchy and rough.

A siren blared. I was moving. Fast. Something covered my mouth. My ribs were on fire, pain knifing through them. My chest felt as if it was exploding.

The pain.

I closed my eyes again.

More black.

Through little slits, I stared upwards at fluorescent lights and white. My eyes felt so itchy and my mouth was unbelievably dry. I turned my head to get away from the light and saw shiny metal railings and a tube snaking out from a pole and into my hand, held into place with tape.

"Samir," said a familiar voice. It was my mother with her thick Bosnian accent.

I didn't answer because I couldn't. I just stared at her. She touched my face, lightly with her fingers, then she pushed a strand of hair off my forehead.

"Samir," she repeated my name. "You awake?"

I swallowed and closed my eyes, not able to answer her. I could hear her breathing beside me. I slowly peeled my eyes open again, this time a little quicker, and it almost felt as if I was ripping a band-aid off my skin.

"He awake," I heard her say. She leaned over the starchy white bed I was in.

Now my father leaned over the bed too. "Oh, this so good," he said. He sounded as if he might cry. My dad? Cry?

"What's…wrong…?" I could barely get the words out.

My dad looked at my mother and neither of them spoke. Then my mother put her hand to her chest and said, "You talk. This good."

"…with me?" I had to finish my sentence, my thought.

"They run test," said my father.

"What?"

"Heart test," said my father.

Heart test? I inhaled and closed my eyes again, but this time I closed them so I could think. A blank page was all I could see. Nothing. I lay still. Then…I thought I remembered playing basketball in the gym with Stuart.

"Basketball." I mumbled. I rolled my head and saw the white cup on a metal tray beside the bed. "I'm thirsty."

My mother picked up the white Styrofoam cup, bent the straw, and put it on my lips. I sucked at the straw, the water a small relief.

"What you remember?" my mother asked.

"Basketball," I said. I didn't want to answer questions. As I sipped the water, a nurse came over to my bed.

"He remember," said my mother to the nurse. "He talking." Then she turned back to me.

I shook my head. I'd been in and out, and I remembered being wheeled through the hospital. But before that, all I could remember was being with Stuart.

"Game?" I managed to squeak the word out.

"The game was cancelled," said my father.

I tried to think. Cancelled? What was cancelled? Why couldn't I remember?

The nurse smiled at me. "We're running a couple of tests on you," she said. "An echocardiogram and an electrocardiogram. I'd also like to ask you a few questions."

Next thing I knew I was telling her my name, what my birthdate was, what school I went to—all questions I actually could answer. But I was hazy on what exactly had happened. I could only remember playing basketball with Stuart in the morning.

Once I'd been prepped with gel, electrodes were stuck to my chest. I'd had an EKG before, so I knew the drill. And the echocardiogram was an ultrasound, again more gross gooey gel. Finally, they cleaned me up.

I have no idea how long the testing lasted, but I was tired from the fussing by the time it was all done. My parents stayed with me. Then I was wheeled out of the ICU and down to another room. Once I was transferred onto another bed, I settled back into the starchy pillow.

"Do you have my phone?" I asked

"Elma have it," said my mom.

"I want to sit up."

My mother fiddled with the remote beside my bed and it was all I could do not to just snatch it from her hand and do it myself. But I didn't. I guess I was just too tired. I wore a blue hospital gown and it felt awkward and all wrong and I didn't want my junk hanging out and that's what I felt would happen if I dared to move. Anyway, I didn't even think I could move. My feet felt like rocks were attached to them.

Once my bed was raised, I tried to sit up, but I was so dizzy. I flopped back into the pillow and stared at the ceiling.

Questions spun through my head, but I didn't have the energy to ask them. No energy at all.

The nurse checked my blood pressure, then she stuck the thermometer in my mouth. After it beeped, she took it out.

"98.6. Normal," she said.

"What you need?" my mother asked, fussing around the bed. There were too many people doing stuff around me.

"To get out of here," I replied.

"I happy you talk. This good thing."

Good? I was in the hospital. None of this was good. I didn't reply.

"They save you."

"Saved?" My mind wasn't thinking fast enough to remember being *saved*.

"They have AED in gymnasium," she said with almost an air of authority. "And they get your heart start, right in gym."

A defibrillator? I knew we had one in the gym because we'd all been shown it during class, and I'd done a CPR course in the past.

Since the nurse was still hovering around me, I asked, "What did those tests say is wrong with me?" I croaked out the words, directing them at her. A defibrillator meant my heart had done something not normal. Not normal at all.

"Your vitals are good," said the nurse, "but I'm going to let the doctor give you the complete assessment and answer all the important questions you may have."

"Can you tell me *anything?*"

She looked me square in the eyes. "Your heart stopped, and you're a lucky boy that it restarted." Then she picked up her clipboard and left the room.

This news that I didn't die should have made me happy, I get that. But it didn't. My head grew heavy and I sank back into the sterile pillow. My heart had *stopped*? Seriously? I was fit, young, an athlete. This heart-stopping stuff was for old people, smokers, and fat guys with big beer bellies. I was a kid who could run for hours.

"I wanna go home," I said.

"What I get you?" my mother asked. Even though she was standing right beside my bed, her voice sounded as if it was coming out of a tin can. "You hungry?"

"No."

"He need good food," said my mother, and I guessed she was speaking to my father, whose accent was almost thicker than hers. They both had a hard time with pronouns and saying the "*th*" sound. They often slipped back into Bosnian, which was natural for them but not so much for me.

"*Ostavi ga*," said my dad, telling my mother to leave me alone. "*Pusti ga da jede kasnije.*"

He was right. I would eat when I wanted to.

The conversation about me eating continued across my bed. "*Mora ke je gladen*," said my mother.

"I'm not hungry, Mom," I said.

They nattered back and forth over my bed for a few more minutes, while I lay with my eyes closed. My mother was going on and on about food. My father kept telling her to shush and he needed to phone my sister and let her know I had finished the tests and was out of ICU and in a room. Wasn't she waiting in the hallway? What time was it anyway?

Fatigue seemed to cover me, squeeze me, but it wasn't like being tired after playing basketball. This was a heaviness, a load. I felt as if my body was detached from my mind. Was I going to be "that kid" with a heart problem? Could it be fixed?

What if it couldn't be? Fixed, that is.

My mother continued fussing around me. I opened my eyes and stared at her. She saw me and said, "You need food. Food make you feel better."

My mother had this thing about food, after being in a refugee camp for five years to escape the war in Bosnia. My sister had been born in Bosnia and spent her early years, from age three to eight, in the camp located in Berlin, Germany, but I'd been born in Canada. My mother liked to tell me they had me as soon as they got settled in Canada. She said she didn't want to give birth in the refugee camp. So, I became the lucky one born on Canadian soil, in a hospital. That would have been the last time I'd been in a hospital: the day I was born.

Had my luck just changed? Gone from good to bad?

"I told you, I'm not hungry," I said. Again, I closed my eyes. I couldn't keep them open.

I think I might have been falling asleep when I heard the voice of my sister. "Hiya, little brother."

"*Shhhh*," said my mother. "He sleep."

I opened my eyes. Elma smiled at me as if she knew my parents were driving me crazy. She held up my phone. "Thought you might want this piece of reality."

She leaned over and kissed my forehead. "Happy to hear you've come back to the land of the living."

"Thanks," I said.

She put the phone on the table beside my bed. "I mean that, you know." She spoke softly, joking put aside.

"Okay."

Elma was nine years older than me and was eight when she came to Canada. She had lived in the refugee camp with my parents, with the scarcity of food, in a room that was similar to a dorm room. She says all it had was bunk beds and a sink and toilet. No kitchen. All their meals were made in a communal kitchen with all the other refugees.

Elma spoke three languages: German, English and Bosnian. You'd never know she'd had to suffer at all. Long dark hair, perfect white teeth. I was the guy at school with the hot, older sister.

"You gave us quite a scare," she said.

"So I heard."

"But I knew you'd pull through."

"Thanks."

"You have another visitor who wants to see you."

"One of the guys?" I wasn't sure I wanted any of them to see me like this.

"Well, them too. No, this is someone who has been waiting for you to get out of ICU. Stuart."

Stuart. My Best Buddy. He's also our water boy for the basketball team and I think he's great. The kid has spunk and determination and likes to laugh. He'd convinced me to join the Best Buddies club at school. I enjoyed it more than I thought I would.

I closed my eyes. Did I have the energy for Stuart right now, though? I really liked him but he was chaotic, like a hurricane, running away all the time, doing stuff without thinking of any consequences. I knew it was part of his FASD (fetal alcohol spectrum disorder) but he had moments where he was most definitely a challenge.

"He's been texting me non-stop," she said.

I looked down at the white sheet and the tube running out of my hand, the opaque tape stuck to my skin. "He doesn't have a phone," I said.

"Well, he's got someone else's phone then. Honestly. Same message every time." She pulled out her phone and showed me his text message.

hi elma when i see sam. im stuart.

I cracked a smile. That was so Stuart. Then I inhaled and ran my hand through my hair. "I don't know. I feel kinda tired. Maybe tomorrow." I wanted to see the doctor first. Figure out what was wrong with me. Stuart would ask a million questions that I couldn't answer.

"Yeah, yeah," said Elma softly. "They knew not tonight. But I'll let them know maybe tomorrow?"

"He's not…outside the door, is he?" I didn't want to hurt his feelings if he was waiting for me.

She shook her head. "No, no. He's just been texting me, asking when he can come. It's way too late now." She pointed to my phone. "It's been blowing up." She gave me a little smirk. "Lots of girls. One named Ginny sent a couple."

"You went through my messages?" I tried to glare at her.

"I didn't actually read the messages, but I saw her name a couple of times. You holding out on me? You got some new girl?"

I picked up my phone and scanned through it. Elma was right, I had a ton of messages, and Ginny, this girl from school, had sent a couple. I hardly knew her. I had heard she was on a mission to get me to ask her to grad. She said she got my number from another girl at school, a friend.

"Nah," I said, answering Elma's question. "No new girl." I shook my head. "Man, I'm hoping I can go home. Have you heard anything?"

Elma shrugged. "I think you're in for what's left of the night. Maybe even the week, little brother."

A night was bad enough…but a week? Not what I wanted to hear.

CHAPTER THREE
STUART

Darkness came and I was in the quiet of my bedroom, all by myself, on my bed, which was in the middle of my room to keep me away from the walls. I was trying to sleep, but every time I closed my eyes I saw Sam on the floor. I rolled one way, then the other way, back and forth. I hate the dark. Hate it. Hate it. Hate it. When I was little and still living with my biological mom I had to sometimes go in the closet when she drank too much or had a man over, and it was so dark in there. I always curled up in a small ball in the corner.

Now, my body was doing the same thing it did then, vibrating like a phone going off and it was like the person just kept phoning and phoning. I bolted up, ran to the walls, made a fist and punched. I didn't punch hard enough to make a hole, but then I fired another punch and cracked the plaster, making a little hole. My hand ached, so I held it for a second.

My bedroom door flung open and light shot in from the hallway like a bright laser beam.

"Stuart, that's enough," said my mother.

"I wanted to see Sam!" I punched again, making the crack a little bigger.

"I know you did. But it wasn't possible. You know the consequences of hitting your wall," she said.

"I don't care." She was always talking about stupid, stupid, *stupid* consequences. Didn't she know I didn't care? That's why my bed was in the middle of the room—so I couldn't stand up and punch the wall or draw on it from my bed. I had to get out of bed to get to the wall.

Well, I'd gotten out of bed.

She walked over to me and gently touched my arm. "How about we go downstairs for a few minutes? Have a snack?"

My body stopped vibrating and I didn't have any more energy to punch the wall. "Okay. Pizza."

"I can manage that," she said. She put her arm around me and guided me toward the door. "What happened to your night light?"

"I dunno."

"I'll make sure Dad fixes it while you eat."

We went downstairs to the kitchen. My older brother, Declan, was still up and he was sitting at the kitchen table, eating cereal. He's my biological brother and is three years older than me. We were adopted together, when I was five and he was eight. Now I'm fourteen and he's seventeen. Soon he's going to graduate from high school and get a job or go to school again. We both suck at school, although he does better than me. My parents want him to go to a school that will teach him how to be a mechanic because he loves cars.

We also have a brother, Randy, and a sister, Mary, but they aren't biological and are older and don't live in our house but in their own places. Randy works for some company and wears a suit to work, and Mary is a lawyer and married to a lawyer. Soon, she was going to have a baby, so I'd be *Uncle Stuart*.

Declan slurped at his cereal. I sat down across from him.

"You used my phone," he said.

"So?" I mumbled.

"You have to ask." He wiped his mouth off. Then he got up and took his bowl to the sink. "You wanna play *Madden NFL*?"

"Yeah," I said. Declan loved any video game with sports, but I liked ones with killing, shooting guns. I wasn't allowed to play those games though.

"Stuart," said my mother. "That's not an option for you tonight."

"Why?" I asked.

"You need to get some sleep because I'm going to wake you up early to fix the cracks in your wall."

"Did you punch again?" Declan asked.

I shrugged. "I dunno."

"He did," said my mother. "And he will have to fix it with putty and sand it down like he always does." My mother looked at me. "It's *consequences*. Now, what kind of pizza would you like?"

"Pepperoni," I said. "Why can't we just leave the walls? It's my room."

"Because they don't look very good." My mother stuck a piece of pizza in the microwave and pressed the buttons. "You need to respect where you live."

"Whatever," I said. "But not tonight, right?"

"No. I won't make you do it tonight. I know you've had a hard night." She put her hand on my shoulder and it felt good.

I slouched in my seat. "Is Sam gonna be okay?"

"I hope so." She spoke quietly. "He's in the hospital now and the doctors are taking care of him."

"That was so weird," said Declan. "He just collapsed."

"He's not weird!" I yelled.

"I didn't say *he* was weird," said Declan. "I said *it* was weird." Declan shook his head at me. "The way he fell was weird."

"Shut up!"

The microwave started beeping.

"Declan," said my mother. "Why don't you go to your room? Stuart has had a rough evening. We all have. I want to spend some quiet time with him."

"Okay," he said. "But I'm playing video games and he can't come in."

My mother put up her hand. "Thirty minutes max. Then I want you to get some sleep too."

24

Declan left, and my mother put my pizza in front of me. Then she sat down across from me. "I do understand, Stuart, how hard this is for you. We all have to hope that Sam will be okay. I promise, I'll call the hospital in the morning to find out how he is."

"I want to see him. Dad won't let me go to the hospital."

"Right now, only his family can see him, and *they* might not even see him until later. The doctors are working on him because his heart stopped for a little while. This is really serious. Even if Dad did let you go to the hospital, you would just sit in the hallway in a chair. The doctors wouldn't allow you in his room because they will have to run tests on him. It's better to stay here, but I promise if I hear anything I will tell you."

"Even if it's the middle of the night?"

"Yes, I promise." She held up her hand, and I tapped it. That meant she would wake me up, even though I normally hated to be woken. Sometimes I didn't fall asleep until 3 or 4 in the morning.

I stared at my pizza. "They hurt his heart by pounding on him."

"No, they didn't. If anything, by doing what they did with the defibrillator, they helped him." She squeezed my shoulder. "Do you understand that?"

I looked up at her. "A what?"

"It's called a defibrillator. I think Sam's trainer called it an AED, which is just a short-form name. Sam went into cardiac arrest—that means his heart stopped—so it was necessary to use the machine to get his heart started again. Would you like to look at this on the internet?"

"Sure."

As we scanned through information on the internet about what had happened to Sam, I ate my pizza. My mother talked to me and showed me things like she always did. The AED was actually short form for words that were way too long. It did help me to see that it was something that would help Sam's heart start again.

After I'd finished my pizza, she closed the lid on the computer. "Time for bed."

This time when I went to bed, my room was a bit lighter because my dad had fixed my night light. Plus, my mother put a door stopper in my door, so it didn't close shut on me. It helped a little. Both of them came in and said good night to me.

Lying on my bed, I squeezed my eyes shut and tried to sleep but everything bounced and bounced.

I must have slept because when I opened my eyes again it was morning, and my mother was shaking my shoulders.

"Time to get up," she said.

"No." I rolled over.

"You need to do a little work in your room after last night."

"Last night?"

For ten minutes (my mother put a timer on), I had to putty the cracks I had made on my bedroom wall. My dad came in to see how I was doing before he went to work and we talked about Sam still being in the hospital. My dad was a lawyer too, just like my sister Mary, so he went to work every morning. And sometimes he worked late. I wanted to see Sam, but both my mom and dad said they would let me know when I could go.

My mother dropped me and Declan off at school, and we walked in together. The first person I saw was Justin, the leader of the Best Buddies program. He organized all our events, even the dodgeball in the gym, which was my favourite because I love running and I'm faster than everyone, except for Sam.

"Hey, Stuart," said Justin.

"Hey," I mumbled. Nothing about the morning made me smile.

"How you doing this morning?" he asked.

I looked up at Justin. "Sam's hurt."

"I know," he said.

"He's not going to die?"

"I sure hope not."

"Will he play basketball again?"

"I don't know any more than you do, Bud."

"My parents won't let me see him."

Suddenly the ball rang. My aide, Tony Simmons, came to stand with us. Tony had only been working with me for a few weeks because my other aide moved. I've had a lot of aides. Some of them just didn't like being with me.

"You ready to head to class?" Tony asked me.

"No."

"Come on, let's go." He started walking and I knew he wanted me to follow him, but I didn't want to. I started running, as fast as I could, my backpack thumping against my back. I dodged kids in the hallway, like I was a football player. My dad taught me how to dodge when we played in the park. I heard someone tell me to stop running in the halls, but I didn't listen. I was rounding a corner and sliding, when I smacked into a body. I looked up and it was Mr. Fujimoto, the vice-principal. My backpack slid off my back and landed on the tiles with a thud.

"Slow down," said Mr. Fujimoto. "You know the rules."

I squatted down to pick up my books and stuff that had spilled out, all over the dirty tiles. Tony came up behind me and bent down to help. His face looked red. The bell rang before we'd picked everything up. All the other kids had gone to their classes.

Finally, Tony and I stood up and he handed the last book to me.

"How about we walk the halls before we get started on our school work?" he asked.

I'd rather walk the halls then do schoolwork, so I nodded. We started walking. The halls were now clear of other kids.

"This is how we walk in the halls," he said. "Not run."

I didn't say anything but kept walking.

"Good job on the walking," he said.

I continued walking because I liked that he said I did a good job.

"I know you must be worried about Sam," he said. "Did you not sleep very well last night?"

"My mother made me patch the walls in my room." I ran my finger along the wall.

"Last night?"

I glanced at him out of the corner of my eye. His eyebrows were squished together. They were dark brown, like his hair, which always flopped over his eyes, but he wasn't black like my parents. Once he told me he was brown. That's how he described himself. He had so much hair on his eyebrows.

"She made me wake up when it was dark, and I had to work for hours," I said. "Right until morning."

He shook his head. "That's not good. I'll look into that," he said.

"They won't let me see Sam either."

"Well, Sam is quite sick."

"I want to see him in the hospital, but they said I can never go there. Never."

CHAPTER FOUR
SAM

The sun streamed through the window beside my bed. I woke up, and at first, I had no idea where I was. Then the stiff white sheets rubbed against my skin. The hospital.

My mother sat in a chair beside my bed with her eyes closed and her head bowed. But as soon as I opened my eyes she jolted upright as if she had some sort of psychic power.

"Did you sleep here?" I asked.

She brushed her hair off her face and straightened her top.

"Go home, Mom," I said. "Sleep in your own bed."

"You sleep good?" she asked.

"Okay, I guess."

"They say heart doctor come today."

I nodded. That was a good thing because I really did want some answers.

My breakfast came and went. And we waited. Me lying in bed and my mother talking non-stop. About what? I couldn't tell you because she went on and on like a long buzzer that just wouldn't stop. The day dragged. The nurse came in and out. I slept. In and out.

Elma showed up mid-afternoon and saved me, just when I thought I might snap at my mother. "Some of the guys are outside. Just came from school. You want to see them?"

"He tired," said my mother.

"Send them in," I said.

Elma left and when she returned Cecil and Craig were with her. At 6'4 and built like a ruler, Cecil loped over to my bed, his crazy black dreadlocks swinging with his walk. More of the shy guy and a true ginger, Craig followed, hands in his pockets.

"Hey, Sokolovic," said Cecil. He held up his hand and I weakly slapped it.

"What's up?" I asked.

"What's up with you, dude? You scared the bejesus out of us."

Craig, AKA Ging, (totally lame nickname but it is what it is) stood at the end of my bed, holding his hands together. "Scared is like putting it mildly. I'm still having nightmares."

"I'm okay," I said, hoping this was the truth.

"Game's rescheduled," said Cecil.

I frowned. "Hey, guys, I'm kinda foggy about the game. Can you, uh, fill me in?"

Across my bed, they looked at each other for a split second. Then Cecil spoke. "City championships, Soko. You were hot. Scored the first two baskets."

I nodded. Two baskets? I should remember *that*. I could remember every basket everyone had scored in every game. Significant stuff. Why couldn't I remember that? I licked my lips. "And then I…what…just collapsed?"

"Yeah, you got a breakaway, going for your second basket." Cecil grinned, shaking his head. "You nailed it too. You were hot. We woulda killed 'em."

I frowned. I wish I could remember. "How long did we play before…?" I don't know why I didn't want to say *collapsed* again, but I didn't. Made me seem weak or something. I'd ruined our game. It had been called off because of *me*.

"Forty-two seconds," said Ging, from the end of my bed. "The game's been rescheduled."

"For when?"

They both looked at each other, again. Sideways glances that didn't include me. "Beginning of next week."

"Maybe I'll be okay," I said.

"That'd be good, bro." Cecil grinned and held up his thumb. "We need ya."

Cecil snapped his fingers. "I heard that Coach Shields might make an appearance. To watch you and me, Soko, in action."

"Lucky you, guys," said Ging.

Cecil laughed and smacked Ging on the back. "It's called skill, dude."

Both Cecil and I had been recruited to play for the Fighting Bears next year at the University of Alberta. They were the top university team in the country because they had a coach everyone wanted to play for.

"That's great," I said. I had to get out of here and play in that game. "I'm sure I'll be out by then."

"You work on that," said Cecil.

Suddenly, the room took on a silence as if we'd hit a blockage in the conversation.

Cecil cleared his throat before he said, "Hey, Stuart is sure asking about you. I swear he's stalking me. Every time I turn a corner at school, he's there asking me if I've seen you."

"He wants to visit me in the hospital," I said. "He's sent my sister probably a hundred text messages. And me too." I picked up my phone.

"You're joking, right?" Cecil piped up.

For the first time since I'd been in the hospital, I cracked a smile. "No joke."

Cecil and Ging stayed for another few minutes or so, talking to me about their weekend plans, and basketball practices, and the latest sports stats. Then the conversation turned to girls and grad.

"So, rumour has it Ginny from our math class is holding out hope that you're going to ask her to *grad-u-a-tion*," said Cecil.

I shook my head. "I don't even really know her. Maybe I won't take a date."

"She told everyone in class today you were trending on Twitter."

"Trending on Twitter?" I groaned. That's all I needed was to be suddenly popular on social media. "You're kidding, right?"

"You hit the news big time," said Ging. "Front page of the sports section. Even made CBC."

"I think someone did up some Facebook page for you too."

"What?" I flopped back on my pillow. I hated attention, except when in a b-ball uniform.

Suddenly, a doctor I'd never seen before (but who looked really official) walked into the room, trailed by my mother and father who had been giving me a little privacy with my friends. I guessed he was the heart specialist-slash-cardiologist? He wasn't my family doctor, that was for sure. My parents had said the heart guy would be in later in the day. This doctor's arrival was the guys' cue to leave and my entire family's cue to return. Elma stood at the end of the bed.

"Samir, I'm Doctor Kapoor." He held out his hand and I shook it. "I'm a pediatric heart specialist. How are you doing today?"

"I've been better," I replied. "You can call me Sam."

"Okay, Sam. Yes, I'm sure you have been better. We need to talk about a few things today, all right?"

I nodded but didn't speak because my throat felt like it had closed up. Not a word would come out even if I tried to talk.

He sat down on the end of my bed, all casual-like. "I've looked at your charts and viewed all your test results. You have what is called hypertrophic cardiomyopathy."

I must have been staring at him blankly (I didn't have a clue what that even meant), because he didn't wait for me to say anything before he went on. "It's a thickening of the wall between the left and right ventricles of your heart. So, what happens, Sam, is the thickened heart muscle makes your left ventricle smaller." He used his hands to talk, making little pictures of my heart, of it being smaller and thicker, and I kept staring at his hands instead of looking him in the eyes. He had long fingers and perfect nails that looked like thin pencils with erasers that hadn't been rubbed.

"So," he continued, "it holds less blood. Sometimes that wall can get stiff. That means the ventricle can't relax very well or fill with blood. This in turn can cause high blood pressure, or it can also lead to arrhythmias because the heart's electrical signals are not working properly. Arrhythmias are irregular heart beats. In your case your damaged heart muscle decided to stop during your basketball game because of the pressure you were putting on it." He raised his eyebrows a little. "You're a lucky boy. Many teens have died from exactly the same thing. Your coach and trainer acted quickly."

Damaged. I had a damaged heart. Damaged. Me?

I gave a little nod to show him I was actually listening. Words were impossible.

"The window is between three and five minutes to get that heart started again," he said. "Their reaction time was admirable."

I nodded again. I knew this. I'd been told. I owed Cassandra and Coach Nelson a lot, for sure. I guess hearing it come from a cardiologist made the reality of what had happened hit home. I could have died. Well, in a way I did die for those few seconds. A heart stops, you're dead. Period. End of story. Grave time. They had got my heart started again within the allotted minutes and I *was* grateful.

But now…I had to get back to this, the present.

"We need to implant an implantable cardioverter defibrillator under your skin," continued Dr. Kapoor, using more medical lingo, "in the upper chest area, which will work with your heart to keep it beating at a steady pace. This ICD will monitor your heart rhythm."

I swallowed before I croaked out, "A what?"

"Implantable cardioverter defibrillator or 'ICD.' They're tiny. Once implanted you won't even know it's there." He opened his binder and showed me a picture of the ICD and where it would go in my body. It was small. And being put in my chest?

I didn't say anything as I looked at the diagram, trying to wrap my head around what was happening to me.

"Once you're stabilized," he looked down at his clipboard, "which looks pretty good right now, we can do the surgical procedure." He looked up at me. "We do want to run some more tests on you to see how your brain is functioning before the procedure. We will do those tests over the next few days." He paused for a split second before he asked, "Do you have any questions so far?"

I was more interested in this *thing* that was being *implanted*. Like I was some freak. "Do I have to have surgery for this...ICD?"

"Yes. It's an insertion and you will need to stay in the hospital for a few days after it's implanted so we can make sure it is working properly and to make sure the incision is healing. Of course, you're healthy so I don't anticipate that being a problem."

I nodded. That was good news. I thought about what the guys had said. The make-up game could be early next week. Maybe they could postpone the game until the end of the week. "I might have a basketball game next week," I said. "Could we get it done before then?"

The doctor stared at me for a second, his head tilted to the side. "Sam, I'm sorry but varsity sports are out from now on, especially basketball because of the high intensity. Your heartrate has to stay within a very particular range and, unfortunately, running full tilt down a basketball court isn't in your best interest. In the future, you might be able to play some house league basketball. For fun."

House league basketball? Was he for real?

CHAPTER FIVE
STUART

We entered the hospital and I walked beside my mother. I'd been to the hospital a couple of times, in Emergency: once for a broken arm and once for a faceplant that broke my nose. Both times I'd been running away from something or just running. I dunno.

Declan told me I'd been in the hospital when I was with my biological mother too. I guess she almost drowned me in the bathtub and I had to go by ambulance. Declan told me that he'd run over to the neighbours' in our apartment and told them how my mother was pushing my head under the water, so the neighbours had called for the ambulance. Declan also said that she was really, really, really drunk, and that she screamed and hit us a lot when she was drunk. He said he used to cover my ears all the time.

After she tried to drown me, that's when we were taken away and put in foster homes. He remembers every foster home we were in, but I don't, at least not the first ones. I remember being at the Langfords' and that's when I got good at running. And I remember our very last foster home, the Williams', because that is my mom and dad's house. They are so nice to us.

As we walked through the hospital, I looked up at my mom, and she must have seen me looking at her because she turned and looked at me too. Her eyes were so dark and brown that her whites shone.

"Did you tell your new aide that I made you stay up all night and fix the walls?" she asked.

"I dunno." Now I didn't want to look at her.

"The school phoned me and asked if that was true. If you did tell your aide that you had to stay up all night, it was a lie. I only made you work for ten minutes in the morning, and you had to work because it was a consequence."

"I dunno," I said again.

"Okay. But you understand why I made you fix the walls, right? And that lying isn't good because it can get people into trouble."

"Am I in trouble?" I asked.

"No. I could have been, though, if they didn't believe my explanation."

I thought about that. I didn't want her to be in trouble. Had I said the wrong thing? Oh well. It was over now. No one was in trouble.

We walked a few more steps before she said, "I think Sam's going to like what you made him."

It was a black, braided leather bracelet, and I'd found a cool basketball bead to put on it. The bead was silver plated. I liked making bracelets and necklaces and they were all made of leather strands and were either black or brown. They were *masculine,* as my dad said. My dad wore the bracelet I made him all the time, even with his suit. I was good at making them, just like I was good at running. My mother had given me a bag to put it in, like this gift bag with stripes on it, and I thought it was lame, but she said it was nice to take a gift that was wrapped.

We took the elevator to the second floor, and when we got off my mother went to a desk and asked where Samir Sokolovic's room was. Once the lady at the desk told us, we made our way to his room. My last name is Williams but I've had two last names. My first last name was O'Brien but it got changed to Williams when I was adopted.

"Remember, Stuart, what we talked about in the car. Sam is sick."

She'd talked non-stop to me about how hospitals were places for sick people and not noise or running. Blah, blah, blah. I nodded.

"Good," she said.

The door to his room was open and we walked in. His mother was by his bed and both her and Sam looked at us when they heard us walk in. I'd met his mother before at a basketball game.

"Hello, Stuart," said his mother. To me she spoke funny, and Sam told me it was because she was from a different country. I can't remember which one. Starts with a B. It's somewhere far away, like over an ocean.

"Hi," I said back. I walked over to Sam and handed him the bag.

"Wow, thanks," he said. "You didn't have to bring me anything."

I shrugged.

His mother patted his shoulder. "You have nice visit." She looked at my mother. "I go for coffee. You join me?"

"Thank you," said my mother. She glanced at me before she turned back to Sam's mother. "But I think I'll stay close. It might be better. Maybe I'll park myself outside the door."

"I bring coffee," said Sam's mother.

They both left, and it was just me and Sam in the hospital room. I looked around at everything.

"I want to see what you gave me." He rustled the coloured paper my mom had put in the bag.

"I made it," I said.

He pulled out the bracelet. "Hey, Little Man, I love it."

It was so cool when he called me "Little Man" or "Little Dude."

"Put it on," I said.

I watched as he clasped the bracelet around his wrist. I pointed to the basketball. "I found that at the bead store and thought you would like it."

He nodded but didn't say anything. I'd only seen Sam cry once and that's when they lost the City Championship the year before. "Don't you like it?" I asked.

He touched it. Then he flopped his head back on the pillow and closed his eyes.

"Are you tired? My mom told me that you might be tired and I should be quiet."

This made him open his eyes and sort of laugh. "I bet she did tell you that." He paused. "How's school going? You being cool to your new aide?"

I shrugged. "He can't catch me. He's slow."

"You gotta stop running, Little Man."

"I like running."

Sam blew air out of his mouth and ran his hand through his hair. "I do too," he said. He exhaled again.

Sam and I talked a little bit longer about different stuff, like the guys on the team and school and how I made the bracelet. I told him every step.

Then he asked, "How's Best Buddies?"

I shrugged. "I dunno."

"Didn't you go to dodgeball today?"

I shook my head.

"Why not? You like dodgeball."

"You weren't there."

"You can go without me."

"It wouldn't be very fun."

"If they're still doing that I Can Play soccer event with the other schools, you should go. You'd get to run lots there. Be good for you."

I looked away and stared at the bracelet instead. I didn't want to talk about Best Buddies. Sam was my Best Buddy, so if he wasn't there, I wasn't going to do anything they planned.

"There's things I can't do anymore." He started to spin the basketball bead around. "Like play basketball."

"Why?" My voice echoed in the room. I could feel my body start to buzz. I hated what he had just told me. He *had* to play. He was the captain, the best player.

"You have to play!" And I stared at him.

"*Shhh,*" he said. "Not so loud." Then he opened his pajamas and showed me a sore he had on his chest. It had a patch over it, but I could see that it was a little red. Like a cut.

"See this?" he said.

"What is it?"

"They put something inside me to help my heart. Make it work properly. But because I have to have it, I can't play basketball anymore."

"You're the one who takes the ball down the court and you score and you pass to Cecil so he can score." My words were shooting out of my mouth, like they were on a high-speed chase.

"I can't," he said. "The doc said no."

"I don't want to be the water boy, then," I said.

"Come on, dude. Stay with the team until the end," he said. "They need you. Anyway, it's just one more game."

"NO!" The word just flew out of my mouth. It was on my tongue and I had to say it.

My mother burst in the room and said, "Is everything okay in here? Maybe we should get going. Let Sam get some rest."

Sam put his hand up for me to slap it. "I am tired, Little Man. Your mom is right. You should get going because I do need some sleep. But I'll see you at school soon."

"I'm not going to fill the water bottles if you're not playing."

This time he just said. "Okay. Your choice." Then he closed his eyes as if he was tired. Sam never got tired.

My mother touched my arm, but she didn't look at me and instead glanced at Sam. "Thanks for seeing him. I know this must be difficult for you."

He rolled his head on the pillow and opened his eyes, but he didn't sit up. "Thanks for coming," he said. "Appreciate the bracelet." He held up his fist.

I tapped his fist with mine and then my mom and I left. I didn't talk on the walk to the car or during the drive home. When we got to our house, I went right to the refrigerator, opened it, and stood there.

"Are you okay?" my mother asked me.

"That hospital was gross," I said. "It stunk." I shut the door of the fridge. I could see nothing I wanted to eat. I went to the pantry. "When is Sam getting out?"

"In a few days," she said. "We're having dinner soon. It's your favourite. Dad's going to barbeque steaks and I've got baked potatoes, asparagus, plus apple crisp for dessert. Mary and Randy are coming tonight. And I think she's bringing the spinach salad you like."

I grabbed a couple of crackers from a box in the pantry and munched on them at the kitchen table while I waited for Randy and Mary to arrive. My mom tried to get me to do some homework, but I drew cartoons on the paper instead. I hate homework. Usually I hate school, but Sam made it okay. Now it sucked.

Mom gave up trying to make me do my homework and made me set the table instead. I'd way rather set the table. Randy showed up as I was putting the last plate down. As soon as he walked in the kitchen, he gave me a high-five like he always did. He wasn't as tall as my dad, but he had way bigger biceps than me or Declan. Declan and Randy loved lifting weights together. I sometimes went with them, but I was so small I couldn't lift half of what they lifted so I hated going. I'd rather run, anyway. Randy told me I had a running build because I was so skinny and light. Randy had played football too, like my dad, but quit because he got hurt too many times, especially concussions, which means he got hit on the head. When I was first adopted we used to go to his games. He was in university then.

"How's it going?" he asked. He put a bottle of wine down on the table. "How's your buddy, Sam?"

"I dunno," I said.

"That's okay," he said. "I can ask Mom."

"He can't play basketball anymore," I said. "So, I don't want to help on the bench." These thoughts had been running and running through my mind.

"You shouldn't give up on your team," said Randy. "When you signed up you made a commitment to the team, not just to Sam."

"None of them like me. Except Sam."

"That's not true. Cecil does," said Randy. "I've seen him talking to you. So does that Craig guy. Man, has he improved. Anyway, it's not about them liking you. It's about you doing a job you said you would do. Right?" He arched his eyebrows when he said the word *right* as if he was *right*. Then he slung his arm around me.

I felt the buzzing start inside my body and I moved away from him.

"Randy's right," said my mother. "A commitment is a commitment, and they only have one more game. I think you could do one more game."

Why didn't they just understand? I DIDN'T WANT TO DO THE LAST GAME.

"I won't do it if Sam isn't there!" I yelled at them.

Randy held up both his hands. "Okay. Okay. Sorry I said anything."

Suddenly, I didn't want to be in the house. And I didn't want to talk about Sam. I bolted as fast as I could to the front door, flung it open, and started running down our driveway. I hit the sidewalk and ran, pumping my arms and legs, moving as fast as I could. I could hear footsteps behind me, but I kept running. I had made it all the way to the end of the street before I stopped. I wanted to keep going but my legs felt like jelly. And my heart was pounding. So I stopped and leaned over. My breath came out in gasps.

"Geez…," said Randy.

I glanced at him out of the corner of my eyes. He had his hands on his knees and was leaning over. His back went up and down as he breathed. "I'm gonna puke."

I stood back up. "You didn't catch me."

"No." He stood up too and his face was red and he was still gasping for his breath. "I didn't," he said. "You're fast." He paused and put his hand to his heart. "And I think I'm out of shape. I haven't run like that since my football days."

"I'm faster than you," I said.

He laughed. "You are at that."

All my bad feelings were gone, and I laughed too.

"Come on," he said. "Let's go back. Mom's making a good meal. One we don't want to miss."

We didn't talk as we walked, at least not at first. Then he said, "Have you ever thought of running cross country or track and field? I think you'd be good at it."

"Sam said the same thing," I replied.

We arrived back at the house just as Mary was pulling up in her car. Her and her husband, Lewis, got out and she waved at us. Lewis had hair that looked like the colour of a pumpkin and a gazillion freckles. Craig's nickname was Ging, but Owen's was Red. Mary and him always laughed when they talked about what their baby would look like when it was born. Would it have red hair or black hair? Fair skin or black skin? Green eyes or dark brown eyes? Special mix, she said. She wore a coat but I could still see her big stomach.

"You out for a little walk before dinner?" she asked. She held a bowl in her hands that was covered in tin foil.

"More like a sprint," said Randy.

We all went into the house and I could smell the BBQ. Mary always helped Mom in the kitchen but today Mom shushed her away and asked me to help. Having a baby got Mary out of doing a lot of work. I put stuff on the table and when Declan came down, he helped too. I was coming back into the kitchen, when I saw Mary and Mom looking at something that was on a piece of paper.

"What are you looking at?" I asked.

Mary turned around and grinned. "An ultrasound of our baby. Come look." She gestured that I should come over. Mary talked with her hands a lot.

I went over to them and stared at this black and white piece of paper that didn't really look like much of anything but a big blur. Then Mary pointed to the middle of the picture. "This is our baby." She almost sang her words.

I squinted and looked at it and what I saw was something that was all curled up and looked more like a big blob or a sleeping mouse.

"Look." Mary laughed and pointed to a spot on the paper. "He's sucking his thumb."

My mother stared at her. "Did you just say 'he'?"

Mary nodded and giggled. "I couldn't wait," she said. "So I asked. They said it's a boy!" Then they hugged.

"What's going on in here?" Declan asked as he came into the kitchen.

My mom smiled, such a big smile. "Mary is having a boy."

"Do you want to look at the ultrasound photo too?" Mary asked Declan.

He shrugged, but he looked at it just like I did. "It doesn't look like a baby," he said. I agreed with him.

Once again, Mary pointed out the baby and how 'he' was sucking his thumb. Then Declan said, "Our mother drank alcohol when we looked like this?"

My mother put her arm around Declan. "Declan, she had a problem. But that's why Mary won't have any wine at dinner."

"I hate our mother," he said. "She made me stupid."

"You shouldn't hate her," said Mary. "And you're not stupid. You just learn differently."

My mother picked up the bowl Mary had brought. "How about we sit down at the table and talk about this." As we walked into the dining room (where we ate when Mary and Randy and Lewis come over), she glanced at me. "You coming?"

"I dunno."

"You should hate her too!" snapped Declan.

"Well, I don't!" I yelled back. Declan was always trying to tell me what to do. Why would I hate someone I didn't know anymore? I hadn't seen her since I was little.

"Boys, let's just sit down."

I was about to run again when Randy put his arm around me. "Dad made your steak just how you like it."

I wanted steak more than I wanted to run. But I didn't want to talk about *her*. She had put me in the closet, and it was dark, and she liked to pinch me and squeeze my arm so tight her nails dug in my skin and made me bleed. Why would I want to talk about her?

At school the next day, Justin saw me in the hall and stopped to talk to me.

"Hey, Stuart. We missed you at Best Buddies dodgeball yesterday."

"Sam's not there," I said.

"You can still come. Everyone was asking about you."

I shook my head.

"Okay. We talked about the I Can Play day yesterday. It should be a lot of fun. You'll like it because it's soccer and running."

I shoved my hands in my pockets and still didn't want to talk.

He patted my shoulder. "It's not for another month," he said. "I'm sure Sam will be back by then."

"He can't play basketball anymore," I said. "I visited him and he showed me the thing they put under his skin to make his heart work."

"I had a talk with the group about Sam yesterday, and why he was in the hospital."

"Hospitals stink," I said.

"He told me you made him a bracelet. Sounds pretty cool. Maybe we could do something like that as a group one day. You could show us how."

"I'm not going to sit on the bench if he's not there."

He patted my back. "I know this is hard on you. But maybe you should rethink your role on the team. They still need you."

"I don't want to."

"Well, Sam might not be able to play basketball, but he can still do Best Buddies. That's good news, right?"

CHAPTER SIX
SAM

I heard them before I saw them. Big feet smacking on the waxed hospital floors. Belly laughter. Pumped voices. Loud and slightly obnoxious. Not even capable of being quiet in a hospital because…they were all still on a huge high. My basketball team.

"Hey," I said when they came in the room. I sat up taller in my bed, trying to look excited. But, seriously, all I wanted to do was curl into a ball and hide. "I heard the news." Yes, I was going to try. "Congrats!"

Cecil carried boxes of pizza, our pizza, the place we always went to after games, practices, nights out. Team pizza. The nurses had given them the okay to come see me. Not too long, they said.

I held up my hand and the guys high-fived me. *Slap. Slap. Slap.* With the group of them congregated around my bed, Coach Nelson held up his hand. Immediately the room went silent. The guys all looked at me. Then Coach Nelson handed me a medal. "You led this team all year and because of your leadership, we won the City Championship. Congratulations, Sam."

The guys erupted into whistles and hoots and hollers. I took the medal, and looked down at it, mainly because I didn't want anyone to see how fast my eyes were blinking. Tears. They were there. Right behind my eyes. I'd missed our final game, my last shot at a City Championship final. This medal was for winning the basketball game *I didn't get to play in.*

"Thanks," I said. I touched it, feeling the rough edges of the lettering. Okay. I had to force happiness. We'd won and that meant celebration time. I sucked in a deep breath and looked up.

"Appreciate this, guys," I said. "I heard you killed it. Cec-Man, thanks for taking the 'C.'"

"It was yours all the way," said Cecil. "We missed you."

"Yeah. Missed you too." I couldn't talk about this anymore. "Let's have some pizza," I swung my movable hospital tray toward the pizza boxes.

Cecil dumped the boxes on it and Ging produced some serviettes. The box was opened and hands grabbed. I wasn't hungry. I was happy for my team, really happy, but it sucked, and inside I had these sick feelings in my stomach because I knew this was the end of *this* for me. *This.* This team camaraderie, spirit, energy, guys. All focused on the same outcome. Highs and lows. Drama.

I hadn't told any of the guys that I couldn't play anymore. Especially Cecil. We'd both been accepted to the University of Alberta to play varsity on the best university team in the country. We were supposed to stay together. Room in a dorm. Live the campus athlete life. Win a collegiate championship together. Now that dream was squashed. I didn't even know if I wanted to go to that university. Why should I? I was going to that school for one reason only: basketball. It chose me more than I chose it.

The chatter continued as the pizza was devoured. No one noticed that I only ate one piece. Even that amount sat like lead in my stomach. The guys rehashed the game and I listened. I chimed in here and there, asking questions.

Finally, a nurse strolled in. "Boys, I know this is a big night, but it's time to shut the party down."

Coach Nelson nodded. "Okay, guys, let's head out. Pizza boxes go with us."

"Rookies," said Cecil. "Your job."

As a couple of the younger guys cleaned up the boxes, Cecil stood beside me. He held his hand to his ear, miming a phone call. "Tomorrow," he said.

I nodded.

He squished his eyebrows together and stared at me. "You're gonna be okay, bro."

I sucked in a deep breath and held up my thumb. I knew if I tried to speak, my voice would crack.

After everyone left, the nurse said, "So, your chart says you're leaving us tomorrow."

"Yeah," I said. "I can't wait."

"I bet you can't. It was nice of your team to come by."

"I hope they weren't too loud," I said,

"They were fine. Short and sweet. Big night for everyone. My daughter went to the game."

"Yeah." I got the word out before my throat clogged. I turned my head. I couldn't let her see my eyes. Big night all right, and I'd missed it.

She finished doing what she was supposed to do and left me alone. I picked up my phone and checked all my text messages. I had ten from Stuart. Obviously, he was using Declan's phone.

I leaned my head back on the pillow. I didn't want to go back to school tomorrow. I didn't want everyone asking me questions, treating me like some invalid, or worse, like some hero, snapping photos to make me "trend" again. The only thing I wanted to "trend" for was scoring baskets, winning championships. And I didn't want to go to the pep rally on Friday where they would raise the City Championship banner to the ceiling. I know, I know—that's a horrible attitude. But it's how I felt. Was I pissed that I didn't get to play? That's a given. Was I happy my team had won? Of course. That's a given too. But did I want to join all the celebrations that went with the win? Not really.

I looked at Stuart's text message and fired one back to him.

not sure when I'll be back at school, bud.

Okay, so there was another thing I didn't want to do. And that was be in the Best Buddies group. I probably wouldn't even be able to play dodgeball. Tomorrow I would text Justin and tell him I was out.

Bright and early, my parents picked me up at the hospital. Elma was working, otherwise I'm sure she would have been there too—a family thing, "the more the merrier," y'know?—but I was relieved to have one less person around.

"You fine?" My mother studied me anxiously. My father had gone to pull the car up to the curb where I sat in my mandatory wheelchair, like a weakling.

"Yes, Mom, I'm fine." I had made a pact with myself to try really hard not to snap at her. I knew she was only trying to help, even though that whole nurturing, food thing was annoying. But I understood After all, I wasn't the one who'd had to live in a refugee camp for five years.

"You smart boy to stay home," she said.

I had told my parents I needed the day off. I wondered if she'd feel that way when I told her I wanted to stay home for the rest of the week. Maybe even for the rest of my life. Couldn't I do online schooling and still graduate?

I sat in the back seat and stared out the window all the way home, not saying a word. When we got home, my father insisted on taking my belongings into my room for me, like I couldn't carry a bag. I was the one who carried stuff for him. I was the kid, the strong, capable one.

After they had *finally* vacated my room, I sat on the end of my bed. Just sat there. My room was full of posters of basketball players. I stared at Steve Nash, the sweat in his hair and that determined look on his face. I'd always wanted to be like him. I told myself if he could do it, I could do it. Trophies lined a shelf my dad had put up; photos of me winning MVP awards were in frames my mother had bought at Walmart.

Then I spotted the letter, sitting on my desk. My acceptance letter from the University of Alberta. Plus, a confirmation letter from the coach there, with the varsity schedule for the fall, including summer training.

I got up, went to my desk and picked up the letters. Swells of rage surged through my entire body. It was over. Before it even began. I wasn't going to play varsity basketball. I wasn't going to play basketball again! Ever. Never.

I started ripping the letters, and ripped and ripped and ripped, faster and faster. Until my carpet was covered with small pieces of paper. My body shook, and hands kept moving until there was nothing left to rip. Then I looked up and spotted the medal my team had given me last night, sitting smack-dab in the middle of the shelf. My dad must have just placed it there.

The one for the game I hadn't played in—for the game I'd wanted to play in since I started high school.

I didn't want to look at it. I didn't want it on the shelf. It didn't belong there and I didn't deserve it. Heat flushed my face. I gritted my teeth. Something was seriously bubbling over inside of me.

I picked the medal up and hurled it against the wall. It pinged and fell. And because it felt so good to throw something I picked up one of my other trophies. I didn't care which one. I hurled it as hard as I could at my wall. Plaster crumbled, specks of white flew through the air like snow. I picked up another trophy. This time I threw it harder. More crushed plaster and this time, a hole the size of my fist. My father opened my door just as I was picking up another trophy.

"Samir?"

The sound of my father's voice made me drop the trophy to the carpet. What was I doing? I was acting like Stuart when he was having a meltdown. What was wrong with me?

All the anger I had been feeling over my stupid situation just dissolved and my throat closed up. I could hardly breathe for a minute. Then, it was like a hose got turned on, and tears streamed down my face. They were fast and furious, and my shoulders started shaking and shaking and shaking.

I just couldn't stop crying. I gasped for breath. My knees buckled, and my father caught me in his arms. I allowed him to take me by the shoulders and guide me to my bed so I could sit down. I wrapped my arms around my aching stomach, rocked back and forth, and cried. Like a stupid baby. Just cried.

All my dad did was sit beside me, with his arm around my shoulder, and let me cry. Snot dripped out of my nose. Salty tears made blotches on my sweats. Finally, I stopped and it was all I could do to catch my breath.

I heard my mother whispering something. She must have been standing at my door. Watching. "Oh, Samir," was all I heard her say.

"He be fine," said my father. He gave my shoulder a squeeze. "He alive and we blessed."

I wiped my nose with my sleeve. Without looking up, I saw the tissue and felt my mother beside me, sitting on my other side.

"Son," said my father, "my first day in refugee camp, I cry like you. Cry till I cannot breathe.

My dad, cry? He never cried. In my entire life, I'd never seen him cry even once. I saw him cut off his finger and he didn't cry. He picked it up, had my mother put it in a plastic bag, and carried it to the hospital so they could sew it back on. This "crying" story, from a world I didn't even know, made me look up and stare at him.

He looked right into my eyes. "I cry like you." Now he turned his head and looked to the ceiling as if he was remembering back. Another thing about my father was he never talked about our family's time in the refugee camp. Said it wasn't important to remember that time anymore.

My mom talked about it and so did Elma. But not Dad. He always said life was moving forward, not remembering backward.

"I was man. I was to protect family," he said, "but we were in god-awful camp." He almost spat his words out. I saw his fists clench and his eyes harden.

"To me," he continued and patted his chest, "I was no man if I no protect my family. I hate what they do to our country. Because there was me, in camp, no house, no food, and a woman and baby." He swallowed, and his Adam's apple bobbed up and down. Then he inhaled and exhaled. I knew he wasn't finished.

"But, after I cry, I work hard to get family out. We were alive, and that count for everything." He nodded his head and turned back to me.

Then in an unusual gesture, he touched my cheek with his fingertip, to wipe away a tear. "You do same." His words were almost an order, but not quite. "My son, you alive."

I swallowed. His eyes stared directly into mine. And then I nodded.

"We happy you alive," said my mother softly.

"I know," I whispered.

"This pass," said my dad. "You live with it." He stood up and his back was straight. "You must."

"I know that too," I said. This time I used the tissue my mother had given me to wipe my nose. "I'm tired," I said. "I think I'll sleep for a bit."

I lay down on my bed and curled into a ball. "I'll fix the wall when I get up," I said to my parents as they were leaving. "I promise."

I slept and when I woke up it was two o'clock. My eyes felt all puffy and my nose was plugged.

My phone vibrated so I picked it up. I had a gazillion text messages.

Cecil, Craig, other teammates, Coach Nelson, Justin and one from Stuart. That Ginny girl had stopped texting me, which was a good thing because grad was not on my mind. I would answer the important ones.

First was Coach.

i'll pop by your office tomorrow

After my embarrassing breakdown, I decided that, yes, I would go back to school, face my fate, but that didn't mean I had to have school spirit or get back to my old life. It was gone. I would function at school and that was it.

Okay, now for Stuart. How was he going to take the news about me quitting the Best Buddies? School was one thing, and right now it was going to be my only thing. I would still be his friend, sit with him at lunch, play games with him, but I didn't want to be in the Best Buddies club. I didn't want to be in any club at all.

see u tomorrow

I needed to warn Justin he'd need to find a new Best Buddy for Stuart, so he was next on my list.

can we meet tomorrow?

Then I sent a message to Cecil and the gang, telling them I would see them all in the a.m. Text messages completed, I lay back down on my bed.

"Come on," I said out loud. "Get up. At least get your butt to the family room and the television."

I pushed myself to get off my bed and went downstairs. We lived in a simple split-level house, so we had a small television room in the lower level. It wasn't a big house, but my parents loved it. I'm not going to lie—sometimes it embarrassed me. But then I tried to think of their side. I'd seen photos of when they had arrived in Canada and how they were met at the airport and given paper bags full of winter clothing. Even with his engineer background, my father felt lucky to land a job working in the shipping department at a furniture company and he never left. He just kept working hard and got a few promotions, so he could provide a home for his family. All my parents cared about was living close enough to the school so we could walk there and get an education. Me and Elma.

When I got downstairs, my dad was in the family room and so was Elma.

"Hiya," she said.

I gave her a little wave.

"Mom's cooking like crazy," she said.

"I can smell," I said. "How come you're not at work?"

"Night shift," she said. Elma had graduated university and was working as a nurse. She had her own apartment but came over sometimes, especially to eat and take home all the leftovers.

The rest of the evening dragged, and I felt as if my family were being too nice to me, wanting to make me happy, trying to make me happy.

Was that what school was going to be like?

I awoke to sunshine. I might have preferred rain. I got up, got dressed, and headed downstairs. My mother usually drove me because she started at 9:00 at her job as a receptionist in a dental office, and school started at 8:30. In the car we didn't talk much although I know she wanted to. She was trying to be all positive and nice, and I guess I might not have been responding.

When we pulled up in front of the school, Stuart was waiting for me. My mother waved to him. She'd met him at one of the events and liked that I belonged to the Best Buddies club. I would have to break it to her that I was going to quit. Like, *today* I was quitting.

"See you tonight," I said, opening the car door. "Thanks for the ride."

"Dad say he pick up."

"He doesn't have to. I can walk. I'll text him." I got out of the car and shut the door before she could say anything more.

Stuart rushed over to me. "You're back," he said. "School sucks without you here."

I showed Stuart my wrist. "Wore my bracelet," I said.

"Cool." He nodded and smiled. "My dad and brother Randy wear theirs all the time too."

As we walked into Sir Winston Churchill Secondary, Stuart kept the conversation going by talking about music and video games, asking me if I'd heard about different rap songs he liked or if I'd played this video game or that video game. I listened and answered his questions. I wasn't a huge gamer so didn't know a lot of the games, unlike Stuart who would play all day long if he was allowed.

Although I didn't want to be the centre of attention, I was. Guys who weren't even my friends high-fived me. Girls smiled at me like I was the puppy in the pet store. That girl Ginny, who had sent me a few texts, smiled at me like I was a celebrity, and boy, did it make me uncomfortable.

When Stuart's aide, Tony, came to get him, I had the feeling Stuart was going to bolt. I touched his arm. "Go with Tony, Little Man. I'm going to class too."

The bell rang and Stuart slouched his shoulders, but he went with Tony.

The good news was that all the attention on me only lasted until morning break because some guy who was part of the druggie crowd got caught with a knife in his backpack and the cops were called to the school. Everyone was talking about that instead. Oh, and Susanna, a grade twelve who was destined to be the valedictorian, kissed Brenda right in the middle of the main hallway (like a lockdown kiss), and that was a topic of conversation as well.

At lunch, I entered the cafeteria and saw my basketball team sitting together. I also saw Justin with Madeline, from Best Buddies, and there were a few others at their table. I didn't see Stuart, but he often ate in a special room or with me. Justin waved to me. Cecil also heckled me, and I gestured to him I'd be there in a minute. Then I went over to see Justin, and the kids from Best Buddies. I still hadn't talked to him about quitting, but I would. Just not in front of the others.

"Hey," I said.

"Join us," said Justin.

I thumbed in the direction of the Cecil's table. "I'm sitting over there but I came to say hi."

"There's a meeting tonight," said Erika. I had totally forgotten about the meeting. Erika squinted at me and smiled, and I had to smile back. She had been born with Down syndrome and she did that to people, made them smile.

"To talk about the I Can Play day," said Gloria. She had FASD, like Stuart, but she also had cerebral palsy, and she was pretty funny at times. I didn't see her Best Buddy, Willa, who was in a rock band and wore the weirdest clothes. Where some girls wore tight stuff, Willa wore bagged-out duds. The group was not something I ever would have joined had it not been for Stuart, but I found out I liked it. A lot.

But right now, I had the energy for nothing, and I certainly had no desire to attend a meeting on the day I just returned to school. I wanted to go home and go to bed. The I Can Play event was sports oriented and I didn't want reminders of my "new limitations."

I know, I know, be grateful and all that. Wasn't feeling it.

"Yeah, we'll talk about that and a few other things," said Justin. "I saw Stuart earlier and he said he was coming for sure."

I cleared my throat and leaned in toward Justin. "I'm, uh, gonna have to quit Best Buddies," I said quietly.

Justin frowned slightly as he turned away from the others to face me.

"That's too bad," he said. "Are you sure? I mean, I can try and look for someone else, I guess. But, look—why don't you give it a week? See how you feel."

"Maybe. I dunno. Anyhow, I'll try and find Stuart to tell him before the meeting tonight. And if I can't find him, I'll text Declan." I straightened up and jerked my head toward the basketball team table. "I should go see the guys," I said. "Make my rounds."

Everyone at the Best Buddies table either waved or said good-bye, and I backed up a few steps, before turning my back on them.

As soon as I got to the basketball table, Cecil stood and held up his hand. "Hey, Bro. What gives?"

I shrugged. "Not much. What's up with you?"

"We're talking par-tee. Friday, dude." He used his entire body to talk. "Cel-e-bration time."

"Cool," I said, trying to sound a little enthused. I hadn't told any of the guys I might not show up.

"I heard there's a band," said one of the guy's girlfriends. She almost squealed. "That is so exciting. I can't wait!"

"It is going to be epic," said Cecil.

Epic? I had to get out of this one. Somehow.

CHAPTER SEVEN
STUART

All day, I was pumped up because we had a Best Buddies meeting and Sam was back. I didn't get to see him during the day though because *Tony* made me stay in the room and do work. And so did my teacher because I didn't do it at home. Don't they know I don't care? It is hard for me. I hate it. Are they all morons? Plus, having to do work I *didn't want* to do and waiting to go to a meeting I *did want* to go to wasn't a good combination because I couldn't concentrate. I kept breaking my pencil so I wouldn't have to do it.

I tried to run too, but Tony blocked me. I wished I had Claire back as my aide. She was slow and had bad reflexes too. I mean, I could start running—take three steps!—before she took her first step. Plus, I was agitated (my mother's word) because I had to meet with the school counsellor, and my mother and father came in too, and we talked about why I said my mother made me work all night to fix my bedroom wall. I don't know why. I wished people would stop asking me stuff like that all the time. Don't they know I don't know the answers, and when I say, "I dunno," I mean it?

I wished I could punch more holes, right in the school wall but most of those walls are cement blocks. Now that would be stupid. I wanted to use Declan's phone to text Sam and tell him I was going to the meeting, but he wouldn't let me, and I only got to see Declan in the morning.

As soon as the bell rang, I ran to the meeting, like, *ran* until I was out of breath. And that takes a lot for me. When I got to the room, I didn't see

Sam. I frowned, pushing my eyebrows together, because he always beats me to the meeting.

"Glad to see you're here," said Justin. He patted my back. "I know it's hard to be here without Sam."

"Sam's back," I said.

"He's not coming tonight," said Justin. "Didn't he talk to you?"

"He's not coming?"

"I'm sorry, Sam. He's not." Justin had a sort of unhappy look on his face. "He can't do Best Buddies anymore. At least, not for a now. But we're glad you're here."

"I don't want to be here if he isn't!"

"Stuart, we can find you another partner. I'll start looking right away."

"Sam said he would be here!"

"How about you hang out with me and Madeline today?"

"NO!"

"Okay," said Justin. "How about Anna and Harrison then?"

There was no way I wanted to be at Best Buddies with anyone but Sam. And there was no way I was going to stay here without him.

I started running. Right out of that room. My legs took long strides and I pumped my arms and ran as fast as I could out the door and down the hall. By now the halls were mostly empty, so I didn't have to do my football dodges. Footsteps sounded behind me, but I kept running, pumping, pumping. I hit the front door, pushed it open, jumped off the steps and didn't stop.

Outside, there was a whole bunch of kids from school and they were running around the track. Sam was the fastest runner in the school last year. He said I should run track and field. I knew if I stopped and ran with them, I might get caught by Justin and I didn't want to go back to the Best Buddies meeting.

So, I ran away from the track, even though I bet I could beat some of those kids, and out of the school yard. Then I went down one street and up another.

Finally, after who knows how long, I was totally winded, so I stopped running. I bent over like Randy did the other day, and I knew what he meant when he said he wanted to barf. But I didn't barf. I just kept breathing and breathing until my heart wasn't banging against my shirt anymore. Then I stood up and looked around.

Where was I?

I glanced around but didn't recognize anything. Where was the school? I needed to go back to the school. I started walking, hoping I was going in the right direction.

A metallic blue car that had two exhaust pipes slowed down beside me. What a cool car! Like, *really* cool. Declan loved cars like this, and he had shown me so many photos on the internet, so I knew it was probably a 2015 Corvette Stingray. I couldn't wait to tell him about it!

The driver slowed to a stop and slid the tinted window down. "Hey, kid."

"Whoa. Nice car," I said. I didn't look at the driver because I was still looking at the car. The paint job was like this shiny blue, that shone, and all the windows were tinted, and it had drag wheels in the back.

"It goes like stink," said the guy.

I turned to look through the window, which was now all the way down. The guy leaned across the seat so he could see me out of the passenger side window.

"You like it?" he asked.

"Yeah."

"You want to go for a spin? I could take you around the block." He opened the door for me.

"Sure!"

I got in the open door and slammed it shut. I pressed my hands against the leather seats, liking how they felt so smooth and cool, like cool as in weather, not just funky cool. I inhaled and smelled the leather and also the Christmas tree smell. I saw the little tree swinging from the rearview mirror and a bunch of beads too. All coloured ones.

"My dad has this smell in his car too." I touched the beads, clanging them together. "But none of these."

"Got those in New Orleans," said the guy.

"You're been there? Wow," I said.

"Happening city. Is your name Stuart?"

I glanced over at him. How did he know my name? Oh well. He did. It made me feel good that he did.

He stuck out his hand. "Donny. Glad to meet you, Stuart."

I looked at his hand, and saw the forest scene tattoo that wound all around his arm. A snake was all twisted in the trees.

"I like your tattoo," I said before I shook his hand.

He pulled up his shirt sleeve and showed me the rest of the tattoo and the snake actually had a tongue sticking out of its mouth.

"Would you like a tattoo of a snake like this?" he asked.

"Sure," I said.

He pulled his shirt down. "One day, maybe," he said. "If you do what I tell you to do, we could get you one. They're special. I only allow special kids to have this special tattoo."

"Can my snake have a tongue like yours?"

"Maybe. You have to earn it. You need a ride somewhere?"

Now, instead of looking at his tattoo I stared at this guy who said his name was Donny, but just out of the corner of my eye, though. I think I recognized him from school, but I wasn't sure. Maybe he just hung around sometimes? He had really blond hair, like, it looked dyed (Declan dyed his hair once and it looked like that), but I couldn't see his eyes because he wore mirrored aviator shades. And he had big biceps. I could see those for sure, even through his shirt.

"I guess I could go back to school." I paused. I really wanted a good ride, not just a ride back to school. I bet this baby could fly. "But first can we go fast?" I bounced up and down in my seat. "How fast does this car go?"

He grinned at me. "You like Death Punch?"

"Oh, yeah," I said, still bobbing in my seat. Five Finger Death Punch was a band my parents wouldn't let me listen to because it revved me up and they swore a lot. He pressed play and with the bass blasting from his speakers, we sped away from the curb, burning rubber. I turned to see if he'd made skid marks on the road and he had.

"Holy F—!" I yelled.

If they could swear in the song so could I. I screamed the word over and over and over. Donny laughed.

His car made this awesome sound, like it was a race car. We drove down a few side streets before we hit the exit for the highway. He made a really sharp turn to get on the highway, and I had to grab onto the side of the door so I wouldn't fling into him.

"*Woo hoo!*" I yelled.

He revved it up and we weaved in and out of cars on the highway. I opened my window and felt the air flowing through the car. It felt so free to be going so fast, with the music cranked.

Soon, though, he took an exit then wheeled around until we were back on the highway going the other way. Man, were we cruising fast. I banged on the side of the car and kept yelling swear words.

He laughed. No one laughed when I did this kind of stuff, so I liked this Donny guy already. I think he liked me.

Again, he slowed down and pulled off the ramp, driving with one hand on top of the steering wheel, like guys do in movies. Like *The Fast and the Furious.*

"I'd better take you back to the school," he said. He braked at a stop sign. "But I can't go too close. Maybe a few streets away."

I glanced at my watch. "Too late," I said. It was past 4:00, the time when my mother was supposed to be there.

He shrugged and gunned it again. "Do you want me to take you home?"

I grinned because I thought of Declan losing his mind when I showed up in this car. "Yeah! I want my brother to see this car. He loves cars."

He suddenly slowed down. "Hey, Stu, it's probably better that you don't say you were with me. If your mom thinks I'm the one who made you late she might not like me too much. I know what moms are like. And I like you and don't want your mom not to like me. You should tell her you were somewhere else."

"Okay," I said. He just said he liked me. Did he like me? I thought of all those other kids outside the school. "I could tell her I was at track-and-field practice," I said.

"Good thinking. You're such a smart kid." He held up his hand for a high-five.

I slapped it. He said I was smart. I liked that.

"I can drop you off on the corner by your house. That be okay, Stu?"

I shrugged. "Sure." Did he really like me? He was calling me Stu. I liked that too.

"But, I'll take you out again if you want."

I turned and grinned at him. "When?" My cheeks hurt I was smiling so much. "Tomorrow?"

He lowered his aviator shades and winked at me before he pushed them back up. "It's a deal. I can pick you up after school but let's not meet in front of the school grounds. How about that street behind the school by the recycling bins?"

I knew where those bins were. I nodded.

He held up his fist and I gave him a punch with my fist.

"Don't forget," he said. "Don't tell anyone you were with me. Better that way. Then we can be special friends. Have a secret, y'know? And tell your mom you were at track-and-field practice. That's a good one." He looked ahead at the road. "Now, tell me where you live."

He dropped me off two blocks before my house and I got out of the car.

"See ya tomorrow, Stu."

I gave him a thumbs-up.

"Remember, you were at track-and-field practice." He gave me a thumbs-up back and sped away from the curb, his engine roaring.

I watched him drive away. Man, that had been *sooo* awesome! I ran all the way home. When I got into my house, my mother came right to the mudroom to meet me.

"Where were you?" She had that look in her eyes that meant I was in deep trouble. "And don't tell me you were at the Best Buddies meeting because I talked to Justin."

"Sam wasn't there."

She put her hand on my shoulder. "You still have lots of friends in the group, Stuart. Those kids like you."

"I don't care. I don't want to do Best Buddies if Sam isn't my buddy."

"You need to understand he's just been in the hospital. Maybe he'll be back soon. Justin said there's a great event coming up called I Can Play and he said it would be perfect for you. It's going to have a lot of running."

"I don't want to go to that."

She exhaled, which meant she wasn't happy with my answer. Who cared? Not me. I had a new friend now. A secret friend who had a car. Even Sam didn't have a car. He had to walk to school.

I had to say I was at track-and-field practice. Donny had told me that was a "smart" thing to say.

"I was at track and field," I said. Then the words just came out of my mouth. "I saw the kids on the track and thought it looked like fun, so I ran with them."

She squeezed her eyebrows together so the lines in her forehead stuck out like wires. "You went to a track-and-field practice?"

"Yeah," I said. "It was fun."

"Well," she said slowly, kind of nodding her head. "I didn't go around the back, so that is possible." She stared at me. "Did you enjoy it? Should I phone the coach and see if you can join track and field?"

"Why would you phone?" I glared at her. "Why can't you just let me do something on my own for once? I can do this by myself."

She nodded. "Okay." She blew some air out. "Point taken. I just hope you're telling me the truth."

"I am telling the truth. You never believe me. I was at track and field."

The next day at school I was allowed to go to the cafeteria for lunch instead of staying in the little room to do work. As soon as I entered I looked around, hoping to find a spot at a table with people who wouldn't tell me to "get lost." Today, if they said that to me I would tell them to f— off. I would.

The basketball players were all together, but I didn't see Sam sitting with them. I was standing and looking around at all the tables, trying to figure which one would be best to sit at, when Sam came up beside me.

"Hey, Stuart," he said. "You wanna eat lunch together?"

"Yeah," I said. "Did you bring cards?"

I saw Cecil stand up and wave to Sam and he waved back, but he didn't go over to him. I wished he would because then I could sit with the guys too. We used to sit with them all the time when Sam played basketball and we were both still in Best Buddies. Instead, he pointed to a table that had a couple of empty seats at the end of it.

"Of course I brought cards," he said. "Come on, let's sit there."

"We're not going to sit with the guys?" I asked. "Play cards with them?"

He shook his head. "Not today. They're talking about track and field and spring basketball tryouts. I don't want to talk about all that stuff." He slung his arm around me. "Anyway, I said I was sitting with you."

"You're the fastest runner in the school," I said.

"Not anymore."

We sat down and I opened my lunch. I had a turkey sandwich, carrots and broccoli with ranch dip, and a couple of oatmeal cookies. Boring. I'd rather have pizza or fries from the cafeteria kitchen. I was only allowed fries on Friday. And my mother wouldn't give me money during the week because sometimes I spent it on other stuff like chips and candy, or even buying something off someone. Once I'd bought a joint. That freaked her out.

Sam pulled out a container with something really weird. He often had weird food to eat. Said his mother cooked it. But he ate sandwiches too.

"How was the Best Buddies meeting last night?" he asked.

"Okay," I said.

"You going to the I Can Play day? It sounds as if it could be fun."

I looked at him. "If it's gonna be so fun, how come you're not going with me?"

Sam ran his hand through his hair and he didn't look very good. He actually closed his eyes for a second before he opened them and said, "Stuart, I'm sorry. There are some things I just can't do anymore. Like I Can Play events. But we can still do this...." He pulled a deck of cards out of his pocket.

"I wanna play Blackjack," I said.

"How about we play Snap?" he said. "Last time we played Blackjack with the guys, we got in trouble. Remember?"

"Oh, right. But only 'cause I won money off you and Mr. Nelson found out." I grinned.

We played a couple of games of Snap (and I won both of them because I was way faster snapping my cards down) before Tony showed up. He stood at the end of our table.

"You ready for math class?" Tony asked, smiling.

"I hate math."

Sam stood and gathered up his trash and books and put the cards away in their cardboard folder. "Tomorrow, dude. Same time, same place." Then he held up his fist and I hit it so hard with my fist that he laughed and pretended like it hurt, shaking it and making funny faces.

Last night, my new friend, Donny, didn't make funny faces. I wondered if I should tell Sam about Donny. Maybe they could be friends too, since Sam didn't have basketball friends anymore. I was about to say something when Tony handed me my books. I snarled at him. He was always wrecking everything with school work.

After school, I didn't see Sam again, but I saw Declan. He was looking at his phone and he was scowling. "I want to work at Best Buy," he said. "But I have to fill out an application."

"Best Buy! You'd get to play video games all the time."

He looked at me like I was stupid. "That's not how a job works. You just don't get to play all the time. I'm going home now. You coming?"

I really wanted to tell him about Donny and his car but I didn't. Donny said not to tell anyone we were friends and to say I was at track and field. I shook my head. "I'm going to track and field. Tell Mom."

"K. See ya at home then." Declan shoved his phone in his back pocket.

I went one way and Declan went the other way. As I walked out the back door, I saw all the kids stretching and getting ready to run in the track-and-field club. It kinda looked like fun. But I wanted a ride in the fast car. *Way* more fun. And Donny was my friend and I really liked having friends and no one on the track team was my friend. They probably wouldn't like me anyway.

I went back to where the recycling bins were and saw the car. He'd come! Just like he said he would. I ran over to the car and he opened the door for me. I hopped in and said, "Are we gonna go fast again today?"

"Sure," he replied. "But first I have to run an errand."

We drove down a few side streets, hit a main road, and drove for a bit, going by Walmart, Safeway, Shoppers Drug Mart, Taco Bell and even a McDonald's. Finally, he turned and that made me happy because on the main road there were so many lights that we had to keep stopping. We were in a neighbourhood I'd never been to and a lot of the houses didn't look like my house. My dad always cut our lawn and made me keep my bike in a special place in the garage. Rusty bikes were just thrown around on these lawns.

Donny slowed down until the car was almost crawling, and we were in front of a grey apartment building that had a basketball court off to the side. Guys were playing basketball. I knew none of them would be Sam, that was for sure.

Donny pulled over to the side. He handed me a McDonald's paper bag, the kind you get at the drive thru.

"Run this over to that guy in the baseball hat," he said. I looked out the window and looked at all the guys playing.

"Is he hungry?" I asked.

"You got it, Stu. He knows you're coming. And he's been dying for this burger all day."

"Okay," I said.

I got out of the car and ran over to the basketball court. The guy in the red hat saw me coming and walked toward me.

"Hey, kid," he said. "Thanks." He took the bag and handed me money. "Give this to Donny."

I took the money and walked back to the car. I messed up money all the time when I tried to pay for things. But I looked at the money he'd given me and saw a ten and a five and *a one hundred dollar bill.* Wow! Now *that* I knew was a lot of change back.

When I got to the car, I handed Donny the money. "That's over a hundred bucks!"

"He owes me for other things." He took the money from me, counted it, and put it in his pocket. "Good job," he said.

Had I done a good job? All I'd had to do was run to the basketball court. So often people told me I didn't do a good job, so I liked that he had told me "good job." Maybe now we'd go fast again. "Can we go on the highway now?"

"I need to run two more errands and then I'll take you somewhere even better than the highway."

"Where?" Since the first errand didn't take much time I was okay with that, if we were going somewhere cool.

"Out of the city to some country roads. There I can really crank this baby up."

"How fast?

"Over 180, for sure. Maybe we could get to over 200."

He turned on the music full blast.

"Holy shit," I screamed. "That's so fast!"

CHAPTER EIGHT
SAM

"You go to Best Buddies, like I say?" My mother put a plate of food in front of me. Today it was a chicken stir fry, a meal I used to like to eat on game days. Why had she made me this? Just another reminder of what I wasn't anymore. Everything I used to like, I didn't seem to like anymore. The food in front of me looked so unappetizing: wilting broccoli, sorry-looking peppers, mushy tomatoes. I pushed the plate away from me.

"I told you," I said. "I just don't want to do the program. I don't want to do anything, okay? Why do you keep bugging me about this? About everything. All the time."

"I worry."

"Don't."

"That boy, he like you. Look up to you." She pointed to my plate. "You don't like my cooking no more? This your favourite."

"Used to be my favourite," I said. "I liked this meal when I played basketball." I paused but only for a second. "And for the record, he looked up to me *when* I was on the team."

She put her hand on my shoulder. "Non-sense. He look up to you because you nice to him. Not just for basketball."

I slouched in my seat. I didn't want to hear about how I was letting Stuart down.

She pointed to my plate. "Food still important. Your heart need food."

I pulled the plate back toward me. I forked a piece of chicken and put it in my mouth. Food had always been something I'd devoured. My mother made meals, and I'd piled my plate and eaten. It was kind of our thing, a bond. I thought about how Stuart would laugh at me when I ate two sandwiches to his one at lunch. Mine were always amazing too.

After I finished chewing, I said, "By the way, I ate lunch with Stuart twice this week."

She turned to me, the concerned look in her eyes replaced with softness. "Oh, that good." She smiled at me. "He like you. You good for him. He be good for you too, you know. He teach you to be happy to be you. It not like he have easy life either."

I sighed, exhaling stale air from my chest. Oh man, she always called it like it was. Stuart was happy with who he was. Why shouldn't he be? And look at Madeline from Best Buddies. She fell off her bike when she was eight and damaged her brain, and she was dealing with that. Why was this all so hard for me? Sports *had been* my life. Competition had fueled me. But…but I needed to move on. I guess I just didn't know how.

"I hate that I can't do anything anymore."

"That not what doctor say." She sat down across from me. "He say you play that other way."

"I'm *not* a recreational athlete." I put my fork on the table and stood up. "I think I'll go to my room."

In my room, I flopped on my bed. I had fully expected my mother to follow me, but she didn't, so I just lay there and stared at the ceiling. As of late, this was all I wanted to do. Which equated to a big fat nothing. The ceiling of my room was white: that's it, that's all. White. Boring, old white. Yet, I stared at it for hours.

Inside my pocket, my phone buzzed. I ignored it. I didn't really care who was texting me. What difference would it make anyway? I wasn't going anywhere tonight. All I wanted to do was stay on my bed and sleep.

Sometimes I went to bed at 8:00. 8:00? No lie.

My phone buzzed again. Then it rang. And I knew who it was. I decided to answer it because Cecil wasn't going away.

"Hel-lo," I said, slowly.

"Hey, Soko. Where'd you go after school?"

"Home," I answered.

"I thought we were going to meet up for a few."

"You had track and field."

"Yeah. But we coulda—"

"I had homework to do." It took everything in me to ask the next question, but I did. "How was practice?"

I could hear him sigh through the phone. "What am I supposed to say, man? I know you don't want to hear this, but it was good. Honest answer."

Now it was my turn to sigh. "Sorry, Cec. It's just so hard not to do *anything*."

"I hear ya." He paused. The silence lingered on the phone.

He spoke first. "You, uh, decide on school yet? I wouldn't count U of A out."

"Not happening. Not if I'm not playing. It'll kill me."

"Okay. Okay. Understand, my bro. Let's talk tomorrow night," he said. "Seven. I'll pick you up."

"I'm, uh, not going."

"You're coming. I'm making ya. You're our captain."

"I wasn't that last game. You were."

"One game. That's it, that's all. Come on, Soko. It'll be good."

"Nothing is good for me. Nothing."

"Seven. Not an option."

The next evening, at Cecil's insistence, I got dressed. Elma came home just as I was coming down the stairs, and I was dressed in jeans and a shirt and had my hair gelled. Why was she here again? She had her own apartment but lately, since I'd come home from hospital, it was like she'd moved back in.

"You're here again," I said.

"Just popped by," she answered, trying to be flippant.

"Did mom send you to check up on me?" I rolled my eyes. "The nurse come to check on her little patient. Look, I'm dressed. I'm going out, okay? You can go back to your own life now. Anyway, you're a nurse not a psychologist."

"Wow. Some homecoming I get."

"I'm fine."

She looked me up and down. "Where are you going? Got a hot date?"

"Team party," I mumbled.

"Oh, sounds like fun. Be good for you."

"Whatever." I could feel my shoulders sagging.

I heard her step toward me, and I put my hands on the counter and lowered my head. She put her arm around my shoulder but didn't say a word. My body felt numb, and I didn't want to cry. Seriously. After the one breakdown in front of my parents, I'd cried at least twice more. Elma could do this to me. Make me all emotional. God, I hated this.

I pulled away from her slightly, took a glass out of the cupboard and poured some orange juice. She squeezed my shoulder before she took a step back.

"You need a ride?" she asked.

Feeling more composed, I turned to face her, glass in hand. "Nah," I said. "Cecil's picking me up."

"That's good. Have some fun tonight, would you? For me." She gave me a cheesy smile.

It actually made me smile, a little anyways. "Thanks," I said. "I'll try."

Cecil and I didn't talk much on the way to the party. I wasn't exactly in a talkative mood. When we got to Smitty's, the party had already started. Music blared and kids leaned against the deck railing, drinking from red plastic cups.

Smitty's house was twice the size of mine, and the deck wrapped around two sides. He had a big pool in the back and a yard that sat on something like an acre of land. His parents loved it when he had friends over and we'd had a few team parties here. The red cups were a familiar sight but walking into this party tonight, with a heart issue, made me nervous. Tonight, was my first night out. Sweat was already beading under my pits and on my forehead.

Inside the house, Smitty saw us and came right over. "So good to see you, Soko." He tossed his black braids and grinned. After Cecil had got his hair braided, Smitty had done exactly the same thing.

I slapped his hand and we did a bro-like hug. Then he said, "Kitchen, dudes."

Cecil and I weaved through bodies and into the kitchen, which had a huge island with at least ten stools. Big windows showcased the pool patio. The doors were open and sure enough there was a white tent put up, just past the pool. Amplifiers and guitars and microphones were already set up.

Epic. That's what tonight was going to be.

Ging, Angelo, and a few of the other guys were leaning against the kitchen counter and talking. Cecil walked over to them and I followed.

"What's up?" Cecil slapped everyone's hands. I slapped everyone's hands too but with far less enthusiasm.

"We were just talking about the game the other night," said Angelo. "Oh man, the Raptors killed it." He thumped his chest with his fist. "My team is *hot.* Plus, I got three of them in my pool."

74

I didn't say anything because I didn't see the game. I'd not watched it on purpose. My dad had though. I'd heard it but stayed in my room, trying to muffle the sound. And I'd let my basketball pool slide, not bothering to see if I was winning anything. I'd been avoiding TSN, Sportsnet, and any other sports channel.

"I still think they'll get killed by Cleveland in the playoffs," said Angelo.

The conversation continued and continued, going from basketball to golf to hockey and back to basketball. I probably didn't say more than a few words. If that. I *used* to love NBA basketball. I *used* to love all sports and knew the stats like these guys did. A feeling of sadness flowed through me and my shoulders sagged, my body feeling heavy. I looked to the floor. The conversation went round and round.

Fortunately, Smitty shouted out that the band was starting outside so we should all hit the patio deck. The band was made up of some friends of his brother. They were a local country band and they liked to say they were "up-and-coming." The patio was lit with little lights and looked sort of surreal to me.

The band started and everyone listened to the music at first and then the dancing started. I had drifted off to stand by myself for a few seconds when I smelled flowers or perfume. Suddenly, Ginny, the girl who had been texting me, stood beside me. Known as one of the best-looking girls in the school, her blonde hair hung way past her shoulders, and the jeans and sweater she wore looked darn good on her. But…for me something wasn't right. Was I crazy? All the guys would think so.

"Hi," she said.

"Hi," I said back.

"You wanna dance?" She smiled, dazzling me.

"Um, I'm okay," I said.

"Okay," she said, looking at the ground.

Awkward silence circled us. Now I felt bad. What a jerk. Finally, I said, "Great party. Smitty went all out."

She lifted her head and smiled at me again. "It'll be the talk of the school year," she said. "Well, except *grad*."

"Yeah," I said. I didn't want to talk about grad. Or next year. Was she hoping I would ask her right here? I didn't even know her that well. She was new to our school this year, but had done a good job of inserting herself into the popular crowd.

She grinned, a little glint in her eyes. "I'm going to the same school as you next year. I just got my acceptance. I'll be able to watch all your basketball games. You and Cecil." She did a little dance with her shoulders. "I'm so excited!"

"Um," I started. Better to get it over with. "I'm not—I'm not going there anymore."

She stared at me, her eyes wide. "You're not?"

I shook my head. "B-ball is out of for me so it's not my best option for a school."

"You can't play anymore?" She seemed genuinely shocked. But then again, the only people I'd told were Cecil and the guys, well, and Stuart, but she probably didn't even know he existed.

"That sucks," she said, and I heard the disappointment in her voice. I guess I wasn't what she wanted after all.

"Look, I gotta hit the can," I said. "Talk later."

With my head lowered, I started to weave my way through bodies to head back into the house so I could look for the nearest exit. Cecil saw me and gestured for me to come over to him, but I waved vaguely toward the house. I didn't want to do this anymore, fake enjoyment at being at the party. The kitchen patio door was wide open. I was heading toward it when I felt someone grab my arm.

"Don't go, man. It's *our* celebration." Cecil pulled me toward him in a brotherly hug. "You missed one game, dude. One game."

"It's not that. If it was just the guys, I'd be okay. But I can't stay," I said. "I just can't."

He cocked his head and looked at me. The he placed his hand on my shoulder. "You okay? I'm worried about you."

I shook my head. "I gotta get outta here."

"You want me to find someone to drive you?"

"Nah. I'll walk. Don't worry about me."

"But I do. You're my wing man." He hugged me hard.

Tears pricked my eyes. What a loser. Now, I really had to leave. "I gotta go," I mumbled. I quickly moved through the kitchen and down the hall to the front door.

The house was fairly empty except for the couples who decided to make out in the corners. No one noticed me as I passed through, heading to the front door. It was like I'd suddenly become invisible.

Once outside I breathed in a huge gulp of air. I honestly felt like I was almost hyperventilating. My breath seemed to be so deep inside of me and I couldn't get at it. I inhaled and exhaled, holding my hand to my heart, trying to feel it. Was it still there? I had never given much thought to my heart. It was so weird to think I had something inside of me that was helping me tick, keeping me alive. It was like my heart was fake.

Finally, I blew out a huge breath of air and stood up straight. I only had about two kilometres to get to my home. Shoving my hands in my pockets, I started to head down the street.

I had only gone three blocks when my phone buzzed. Thinking it was Cecil, I pulled it out of my pocket. But it was Stuart. Poor kid. I'd bailed on him. Oh well, he'd figure it out. I'm sure Best Buddies could hook him up with someone else. I ignored the text and stuffed my phone back in my pocket.

CHAPTER NINE
STUART

"This is where you live?"

I stared out the window as Donny pulled up in front of a house. Today we were going to *his* house. The house looked old and worn out, and a little like my messy bedroom, with stuff lying all over the place. Only instead of clothes on the brown lawn, there was a rusty bike, a wheelbarrow, and a winter shovel.

"Not for long," he said. "One day I'm livin' in a mansion somewhere, with a pool and stereo system that blasts music. It'll be in the country too, so I can make as much noise and make as many deals as I bloody-well want."

He got out of the car, so I did too.

"Do your mom and dad live here too?" I shut the car door and just stared at the old house.

He laughed. "It's been years since I've lived with my old man and lady, kid."

"How old are you?"

"Nineteen."

"You seem way older than that. My brother Declan is almost eighteen, and he still lives with my mom and dad. They're not my biological mom and dad but I still call them mom and dad."

"You're lucky." He nodded his head at me. "I never had no one to call Mom and Dad. I just had foster parents and some of them were mean sons-of-bitches."

"My mom drank alcohol when she was pregnant with me, so that's why I got a new mom and dad."

He nodded and winked at me. "I know that, kid. I picked you to run my errands because you're special. And I'm going to make you even more special soon. Lots of time though. You do a few more things for me and you might even get a tattoo."

I grinned at him. He picked me? Because I was special? Wow. How cool. No one at school ever picked me. In fact, I was always the last one to be picked.

Lately, I had run errands with Donny every day after school. He liked that I was a fast runner and I guess I knew it wasn't McDonald's burgers in the packages because they didn't smell like McDonald's. But I didn't care because I had a friend.

And now I didn't even care that Sam had quit Best Buddies and didn't text me anymore. Sam wasn't all that much fun now anyways because he had a stupid, sad face and walked slowly and didn't do anything fun like he used to when he played basketball.

We walked up Donny's front walk and he opened the door, unlocking two locks. When we went in I looked around, and it was nothing like my house, that was for sure. For one thing, the brown sofa wasn't on legs and just sat on the floor. And the carpet was kind of dirty, and had spots where it looked like people had spilled stuff. My mom vacuumed all the time and had the carpets cleaned if they got too dirty. When the carpets were cleaned we had to stay out of the room until they dried. And there was a lot of stuff everywhere, like papers and blankets and pillows, even sleeping bags as if people slept in the living room. There were no plants or paintings on the walls. BUT there was a huge television and lots of controllers for video games.

"You want to play *Kill Zone*?" He picked up the package for the video game and handed it to me. "Or you can also play *Hunting*." He pointed to a package lying on the dirty carpet. "It's a new one that just came out."

"*Kill Zone!*" This was a "forbidden" game.

I stared down at the package in my hand and my body started to vibrate, I was so excited. "My parents never let me play *this* game."

"Cool. I'll set it up for you."

Donny explained the game to me, and I sat down in front of the television. When it came on, I just stared at the screen. I got to kill people with knives, guns, and even explosives if I wanted to. And the best part was, there was no one around to tell me not to zone out. The noises from the game were made super loud by speakers. What a setup!

I played and played, killing people all over the place. I got to hide behind brick walls and jump out at them, knifing them, watching the blood spurt as they crumbled and fell to the ground, gasping, holding their wounds. And I got to rob stores and kill the person behind the counter.

I was just about to shoot a store owner when I felt a hand on my shoulder. "Hey, Stu."

I almost jumped out of my skin. "You scared me," I said.

Donny laughed. Then he glanced at the television screen. "Killing store owners," he said. "Good job. I like that." He took the controller from me. "No more for today. We have to get you home. You do what I say, Stu, and you can play this game again. Next time I'll give you a little something that will make the game that much better."

I scrambled to stand up. If I did what Donny said, I would get to play this game again.

Donny slung his arm around my shoulder. "Remember what I said. This is our special time. No one can know. If you let anyone know, it won't be special anymore."

I nodded. "Okay," I said. Donny had a cool car and cool video games. I needed to do what he said.

"Can I go to the washroom before we go?" I asked.

"Down the hall to the left," he said. "Be quick."

I went down the hall but then couldn't remember what he had said. Left or right? I wasn't great with my left and right anyway. There was a door that was closed, and I figured it might be the one so I opened it. But it wasn't the washroom. The only thing in the room was a table, some chairs and a big thing that looked like a scale, and packages of white powder.

And guns! Guns! Real guns. I wanted to see them. Touch them. What if I put one in my hand and pretended to shoot it? I could pick something on the wall and snipe it just like in the video games!

I went to the table and picked it up. It was way heavier than I thought it would be. And cold. The metal was hard. I wrapped my hand around it and stared at it. Then I pointed it to the wall. *Boom. Boom.* What would happen if I actually pressed the trigger?

"Hey!" Donny stormed into the room. "What the f— are you doing in here? Put that down!"

I did what he said and I put the gun back on the table.

Donny grabbed my arm and dug his fingers into my skin. His eyes had changed and they looked black. In my mind, I saw my biological mother, when I was little. Her eyes used to get like this.

I ducked. "Don't hit me," I said.

He yanked my arm and pulled me out of the room, his fingers still digging hard into my skin.

"Don't," I said. "You're hurting me."

He let go of me, and I rubbed my arm. Red marks were appearing where his fingers had been.

"Don't be nosing around." It was like he hissed his words. "And never touch my guns."

My throat felt really dry and my stomach was turning upside down. "I still have to pee." Now I really had to pee.

He shoved me hard toward another door, which opened and, sure enough, I saw a toilet and sink.

"Go," he said.

I went to close the door but he blocked me from doing that. "I want the door open."

At first it was hard to pee knowing he was watching me, but then it came out. I finished, flushed the toilet, and washed my hands.

He didn't talk to me at all when we walked outside. When we got in his car, he looked over at me. "What you did in there was wrong, Stu. It's *my* house. *My* things. I tell you what you can play with and where you can go." He started his car and peeled away from the curb, squealing his tires.

I wondered if him grabbing my arm was my *consequences* for going in the room.

"We have time for a fast ride," he said.

I glanced over at him and now he was smiling at me, so I smiled back. He wasn't mad at me anymore. He put his hand on my shoulder.

"We're friends," he said. "Don't forget that."

After a fast spin on the highway, a super-short one, he dropped me off, three blocks from my home, and in a different spot.

"How come you're dropping me off here?" I asked.

"Run, kid. You're fast. Keep telling your parents you're at track-and-field practice. And don't mention my house or my room. You do, I will never let you play my video games again." He smiled at me. "You liked those games? Right?"

I nodded. I got out of the car and, because I wanted to make Donny happy and keep the smile on his face, I took off running as fast as I could, which wasn't as fast as I really could because my backpack kept shifting all over the place, slowing me down. Too many stupid books that Tony made me take home.

I kept running anyway because if Donny watched me run fast maybe he'd still like me.

I heard his car and when I looked back, he'd done a U-turn in the middle of the street and taken off the other way.

Didn't matter. I'd still run fast because he told me too and because he was right about my parents thinking I was at track and field.

By the time I got home, I was tired and sweating. The sun shone in the sky and the rain that had happened had cleared everything and made buds come out on the trees, and it was hotter than it had been in days. I stood for a few seconds, trying to catch my breath before I walked around to the back of my house.

When I opened the back door, I heard voices and it sounded like Sam was at my house. He'd only been to my house a couple of times before: once when my parents wanted him to come to dinner and another time when we were getting ready to go to an event and my parents were driving us. I couldn't always remember everything, but I remembered that event. A dance with a disco ball and we did the conga line and danced like robots. And there had been a photo booth where I dressed up as a cowboy and Sam had dressed up as the lawmaker. It made me think about how that event had been a lot of fun too, and that Sam never grabbed my arm when we were friends.

I stood still and listened to the voices. It sure sounded like Sam. I dumped my backpack on the floor and took the stairs two at a time.

"Stuart," said my mother, almost as if she was out of breath. "You're home!" She held her hand to her chest for a second then she reached out and hugged me, which was kind of weird. I'd just come home from school. No big deal.

When we walked into the kitchen I found out I was right. Because sure enough, there was Sam, sitting at my table where I ate breakfast.

"What are you doing here?" I asked him.

Sam looked funny, like he'd been caught doing something he shouldn't do. He glanced at my mother and she glanced at him, then they both looked at me.

"I'd like you to sit down," said my mother.

Uh oh. Had I done something wrong? Was this going to be a consequences talk? I hated that talk. I sat down anyway. Sam sat down too because he'd stood when I came in.

"Sam said he saw you getting into a car after school," said my mother.

I looked at Sam. "You saw me?"

He nodded. "Little Man, buddy, that guy is bad news."

"You know Donny?"

"Donatello. Lots of people know him," he said.

"Look at me, Stuart," said my mother. So I did. "You told me you were at track and field." Her eyebrows were squeezed together and she stared directly into my eyes.

I hung my head and slid down the chair. I stared at the tabletop.

"Why did you lie to me?" she asked.

"I dunno," I said, kicking the chair across from me.

"Can you think about this for a minute?"

"Okay." I still stared down, not wanting to look anyone in the eye. I hated looking people in the eye. My hands automatically moved up and down my thighs, and I scratched. The sound of my nails on the denim kind of echoed because no one was talking.

Why did I go with Donny?

"He has a super-fast car and took me for rides," I said. Then I thought of something else. "And he wanted to be my friend."

Sam blew his breath out, like, super loudly, like he'd just come off the basketball court, only he couldn't play basketball anymore.

"Stuart," he said almost in a whisper, "I'm so sorry."

"This isn't your fault, Sam," said my mother.

I looked up. "Is it my fault?" I sure hoped it wasn't.

My mother blew air out of her mouth too. "Let's not place blame. But Stuart, you can't just take rides from people you don't know. And you can't lie. You lied to me about going to track and field."

"He's not a stranger anymore. I know him now," I said. "Only the first day was he a stranger. He said I was special. Sam didn't want to be my friend anymore, but Donny said we were friends."

"I did so still want to be your friend," said Sam.

I stared at him, and this time I definitely frowned. "No, you didn't. You quit Best Buddies."

"Because I was sick," he said. "And…I just couldn't handle anything but school." He rubbed his hands together and had that droopy look on his face like he was a sad dog.

"You still quit," I said.

"You're right," he said. Then he sucked in this huge breath of air. I just looked at him. He looked at me too, like, right at me. "We can go back," he said. "I can join up again. Let's do the I Can Play event. It's on the weekend. I'll go with you."

"Sure," I said. I stood up, thinking that everything was over.

"Sit down, you," said my mother. "I want to chat a little longer." She clasped her hands together.

I hated when she did that because that meant we might have to talk on and on and on. I was tired of talking and sitting. So boring.

"How about we put on a timer and go for five minutes," I said. That's what she always did to me. Put on a timer when she wanted me to do my homework.

"Fair enough," she said. She got up, went to the oven, and put the timer on.

"Five minutes," I said. No longer.

"Okay." She came back to the table and sat down. I hoped the minutes were ticking by. "I want to know—what else did you do with this…Donny?"

I thought about the errands. And the video games. And the fast driving in the car. Which one did he tell me not to tell? Then I thought about how mad he was going to be because he was going to think I told about us.

"I wasn't supposed to tell that we were friends," I said.

"It's important," she said.

I thought about how he'd squeezed my arm so hard it made marks. I looked at it to see if they were still there. Then my mother leaned over and lifted my sleeve. "What are these marks?"

"I dunno," I said.

"Did he hurt you?" She leaned even closer to look at my arm.

I yanked it away. "No! He didn't hurt me. I went in the wrong room. He was nice to me. He took me for fast car rides." My words just tumbled out of my mouth.

"Oh, my goodness," said my mother. She pressed her fingers to her forehead. "I need to call your father."

My mother got up and snatched her cell phone off the counter. I was so happy when she turned the timer off on the oven and went into the other room.

Now it was just me and Sam sitting at my kitchen table. I was glad not to have to talk about Donny anymore, but it was kind of weird to have Sam at my house because, well, it just was. Friends didn't come over to my house anymore. They used to—kids in the neighbourhood—but not anymore. Not since, like, grade four or something.

"So, what do you think about going to I Can Play this weekend?" Sam asked me. "Your mom said she would drive us."

"Sure," I said. "But only if you are going and we are going as Best Buddies." I twirled a paper napkin around and around and around, until it made me dizzy. Then my stomach growled. "I'm hungry," I said.

We have a huge pantry in our kitchen. One shelf is filled with food that I'm allowed, including taco chips. I pulled out the bag and brought it over to the table. Then I got some salsa out of the fridge. I held it up. "This is the hot kind."

Sam laughed and I sat down and we both ate some chips, right out of the bag.

"I promise I'll go back to Best Buddies," he said, in between bites. "I'll call Justin tonight. How's that? Or..." he pulled out his phone, "we could call him right now."

We called Justin and Sam put the phone on speaker. We chatted for a few minutes and Justin sounded excited that we were coming back. He kept saying how good the I Can Play event would be for me. Lots of running.

When Sam had pressed end, he took another chip but this time he didn't eat it and instead just cracked it into two. He looked at me and said, "Stay away from Donny. Okay? He is bad news. Like, really bad news."

I took a chip out of the bag and ate it without even looking at Sam. Donny had been nice to me, well, except for today when he'd hurt my arm. I looked at my arm and could still see red marks, and they looked like they might turn into bruises.

"He'll give you bruises like that on your face and body if you do something he doesn't like," said Sam. "If you see him again, promise me you'll run as fast as you can the other way, okay?"

I didn't answer but dipped my chip in salsa then ate it.

"I've said enough," said Sam. "Anyway, I should get going."

"How'd you get here?" I asked.

"I phoned your mom when I saw you get in the car and she came and picked me up and brought me over here."

"Mom!" I shouted out.

She came into the kitchen, holding her phone in her hand. "Stuart, what is it?"

"You need to give Sam a ride home."

She actually smiled for the first time since I had got home. "Okay," she said. "Why don't you come with us for the ride?"

On the way to Sam's house, we didn't talk about Donny and I was happy about that because I didn't want to talk about him anymore. But on the way home, my mother started in on me again about him.

"He's a known drug dealer," she said, "and you can't be hanging out with him."

"Okay, okay," I said.

"You didn't do any drugs with him, did you?"

"NO!" I screamed. "I don't want to talk about this anymore."

So, we didn't. When we got home, everyone was at our house, and even Mary was over, even though it wasn't a night she usually comes over.

My mom and I walked into the house together and when Declan saw me he said, "You rode in Donatello's car?"

"His name is Donny." Then I thought about the car. "You should see how fast it goes," I said. "You'd love it."

"He's a drug dealer y'know. Everyone at school knows that."

I shrugged.

"If you hang out with him you could go to jail," said Declan.

"Jail?"

"Declan, that's enough," said my mother.

"I wish we could get the guy on something," said Mary. She drummed her fingers on the counter as if she was thinking hard. "But everything is hearsay and nothing would stick. He'd walk. And this kind of thing could make him turn on Stuart."

My dad shook his head at her. "You're right. We have nothing at this point. It's only Stuart's word. Unfortunately, that won't fly. But he may slip up. I think we should talk to the school and get some sort of street surveillance. They need to know he's cruising around."

Mary took me by the shoulders and looked directly in my eyes. "You're a lucky, boy, Stuart," she said. "Having a friend like Sam." She pulled me in for a hug, but it was hard because of her big stomach.

"You're too big," I said.

She laughed for a second before she got serious again. "You stay away from him, you hear? Run like the wind if he comes close to you."

CHAPTER TEN
SAM

It was Cecil who told me about Stuart and that Donatello guy. On Thursday, when I got to school I entered the front doors, my head down, my hands shoved in my pockets, and banged into Cecil. His hair was wet as if he'd just stepped out of the shower. I stared at him and felt a pang. That used to be me in the mornings, especially in the spring.

"Working out?" I asked.

"Yeah," he replied. "Spring tryouts are on the weekend. Nelson wanted to work with me."

I nodded, remembering doing the exact same thing last spring with Coach Nelson. Early morning sessions before I tried out for spring league. I had juggled track and field (my specialty was the 100 and 200 metres) and basketball.

"Good luck," I said.

"Crap, man. I'm just gonna say it. You woulda been a shoo-in. Angelo's trying out too. Nelson thinks he might make it."

"Seriously? Angelo?" Angelo was good but needed work on foot speed.

"Yeah. Don't think the track team will pack the same punch as last year." He patted my shoulder. "We need you."

At least I was missed. For some reason that made me feel slightly better but also way worse. I held up my fist and he hit it with his. And just like that, the conversation about sports was a done deal.

We started walking to English class. What else could we talk about?

"You get your assignment done?" I asked. Lame conversation. Cecil and I didn't talk about *school work. Ever.*

Cecil nodded. "Done and done. I kind of liked the book I picked. *Three Day Road.* About World War I and a guy who gets hooked on drugs." He snapped his fingers. "That's what I meant to tell you. You need to get back to your little buddy. I think he's gonna be in a mess of trouble soon."

I frowned at Cecil. "What are you talking about?"

"He's hangin' with a *baaaad* dude."

"Stuart?" Stuart's parents watched him pretty closely.

Cecil looked at me and raised his eyebrows up. "I think I saw him gettin' in a car, behind the back of the school. Past the track area. Not good. The guy's name is Donatello Dunn and he was in my brother's grade all through elementary. He's nasty, into all kinds of crap. Gangs, robberies— seriously, he's on a path to jail. He's already spent time in juvie."

"Are you sure it was Stuart?"

"Not a hundred percent. That's why I didn't set off the alarm. But you may want to check in on him."

All morning I thought about Stuart and what Cecil had said. Could he have been mistaken? The thought of someone coercing Stuart made me sick to my stomach, but it wasn't an unlikely scenario. He was trusting and vulnerable and didn't think of repercussions. It's just who he was, how he operated. But his parents kept close tabs on him.

At lunch I waited for him and when he didn't show up in the cafeteria, I went looking for him. I found him in a private room with Tony, his aide, but since he was immersed in his work, Tony didn't want me interrupting. Fair enough.

When the bell rang at three, instead of hightailing it out of the school right away and back home to the sofa, my place of afternoon activity these days, I decided to try and find Stuart. When I saw Tony, leaving the school, I waved him over to me.

"Where's Stuart?" I asked.

"I don't have him last period," he said. "But I think he said he's been doing track-and-field practice."

"Thanks," I said. Track and field? That didn't sound right. Cecil would have noticed if Stuart was showing up at the track. But I figured it wouldn't hurt to check.

The track was located in the back of the school, so I headed to the doors that led outside. Stepping out, I saw a familiar sight. Kids were everywhere, dressed in workout clothing, wearing cleats, running sprints, high jumping.

For a few seconds, I watched the sprinters as they lined up at the start, working on positioning in the blocks. I always used the blocks and crouched low, so I could get explosive power that way. I put my hand to my chest, where my new mechanism had been inserted under my skin. Yeah, it was there. And, no, I wasn't running the explosive events ever again.

I glanced around for Stuart but didn't see him. He would have been with the runners. I skirted around the outside of the track, head lowered, so no one would talk to me or call me over. I got closer to the frost fence that surrounded the school and the recycling bins.

I heard the car before I saw it. Then it came into view. A blue corvette with dual exhaust that sounded as if it belonged on the race track. I picked up my pace and started to jog.

Then I saw Stuart dart out from behind the bins and race to the car. The passenger door swung open and he hopped in. The car took off, squealing tires and leaving rubber marks on the road.

I started to chase it, trying to read the licence plate. BNM were the first three letters. I said them over and over in my head. And kept running. But the car was fast. This wasn't good. I needed the rest of the plate number. I kept running. 3005. I had it.

I stopped running but my heart ticked and ticked, going too fast. Way too fast. I saw stars sparking in front of my face.

I gasped for breath. Dizzy. My legs felt wobbly. My heart felt as if it might explode. My head ached. I kept gasping. And gasping. I bent over at the waist. The stars kept circling in front of me.

Breathe. Breathe.

I had to slow down my breath. I had to. I touched my chesst over my heart. Felt its pounding. Dangerous. The doctor told me I could have died. I was lucky I didn't die. Didn't have brain damage.

I sat down on the ground and wrapped my arms around my knees and slowly rocked back and forth to calm my body down. As I did that, I recited the licence plate. BNM3005. BNM3005. Over and over.

I'm not sure how long I sat on the ground but finally my breath returned to normal. Slimy sweat dripped down the side of my face and coated my forehead. Not a good sweat. More like a toxic sweat. I also had a sick stomach. I squelched down barf and continued to sit.

And think.

Never mind me. I had to do something about Stuart.

I sucked in another breath of air, taking the oxygen deep inside me. Okay, so I wasn't as lightheaded anymore. I was going to be fine. I rubbed my sweaty hands on my jeans before I pulled my phone out of my pocket. I had to call someone. Who? His parents. They were the best bet.

When Stuart's mother answered I said, "Hi, this is Sam." And before she could even say hi back, I said, "I think Stuart's with someone he shouldn't be with." My words came out in a rush.

"What?" I could hear her confusion. "He's at track and field."

"No, he's not."

"Where is he?" Now I could hear fear in her voice.

"He got in a car with the licence plate BNM3005. Have Randy or your husband track it down and see who it belongs to but I'm pretty sure the guy is not who you want Stuart hanging around with."

"Oh, my goodness," she whispered. "And here's me thinking he was at track and field. What was I thinking?"

"Tony thought that too," I said. "Stuart's smart." I paused for a second then just blurted out, "I think I let him down."

"No, no." She sounded really distracted.

"I'd like to be there, at your house, when he comes home," I said. "I need to talk to him. Tell him I'm sorry."

"You have nothing to be sorry for. But I agree. That's a good idea for you to be here. I'll pick you up. It might really help."

I told her my location and then waited. It didn't take her long and I could tell by the strained look on her face that she was as worried as I was.

"Thank you so much for calling me," she said as I buckled up my seatbelt.

"Of course," I said. "A friend told me at school, so I tried to follow him. I couldn't chase the car down." I glanced out the window. I couldn't help my friend because I had a bad heart. What use was I?

She sighed and drove away from the curb. "He's been coming home every night around the time he would get home from track-and-field practice. I was allowing him to walk because I wanted to give him a sense of independence. He had such convincing stories about his practice. Declan even said he saw him going outside in his track gear." She gripped the steering wheel.

We drove on in silence until she turned into their driveway. She flicked the remote to open the garage door and as she drove into her spot, her phone pinged. She shoved the car in park and grabbed the phone as she cut the engine. I sat quietly while she read her text.

"Oh, dear. You were right about that fellow he's with." She closed her eyes for a second before turning to me. "To use your words, this guy is bad news. I just feel sick about this. Why didn't I follow up with the track-and-field coach? I always do."

Sweat slid down my forehead. What if Stuart was in trouble?

"I should have checked up on this track and field deal," she said again, almost as if she was talking to herself. "He's different than Declan. A little more trusting with people. Well, actually, a *lot* more trusting. Always has been. Declan was clingier and much more cautious. I just wanted to let Stuart do something on his own." She turned to me. "Thank you again. This licence plate number is so important. It gives us something. Thankfully, my husband is a lawyer and knows a few police officers." She put her purse under her arm. "I guess we should go in the house and wait."

I nodded, not sure what to say. I got out of the car and followed her into their house.

And wait we did. Her pacing, and talking on her phone. Me, sitting quietly at the kitchen table, drinking a glass of cold water. At 4:25, she glanced at the kitchen clock. "He should be home any minute now."

"Yeah," I said. "Track usually ends between 4 and 4:15."

"It would take him ten minutes to walk home. I should have picked him up instead of letting him walk home. But what am I saying? He wouldn't have been—."

We both jumped when we heard the back door open.

"Go," I said.

She took off like she was a runner coming out of the blocks, disappearing around the corner and into the mudroom. I heard her say Stuart's name, and I heard him talking to her. The sound of his voice made me exhale, like seriously unload a heap of stale air.

When he walked in the kitchen and saw me, he just stared at me. "What are you doing here?"

His mother made him sit down and then it was time for the "talk." I just listened to her telling him how dangerous it was to take rides from people he didn't know. Watching his face, I saw exactly how vulnerable he was, to use his mother's word. He hadn't gone in the car to be bad; he'd just wanted a friend.

I'd bailed on him. A little voice in my head said, "Well, you ate lunch with him." But why did I eat lunch with him? To save myself from having to socialize with my basketball friends. Some friend I was.

After Stuart's mother had talked on the phone to his family about what had happened, she gave me a lift home. In the car, Stuart was happy that we were going to the Best Buddies event. It was as if he'd already forgotten how much trouble he could have been in.

But I didn't forget. I needed to make this up to him.

Saturday morning, my alarm went off and I got right out of bed. After a quick shower I headed downstairs to the kitchen and slurped down a bowl of cereal. For the first time since my heart had stopped, I felt okay. Today, Netflix would have to wait.

When my mother came in the kitchen, dressed in her Saturday morning robe, I was downing the remains of a glass of orange juice while standing in front of the sink.

"You like eggs?" she asked.

"Nah. I had cereal, thanks."

"Take snack."

"I'm good."

My phone pinged and I picked it up off the counter, reading the text from Stuart on his mother's phone, telling me they were out front.

"Stuart's mom is here. I'm off."

My mother took two steps toward me and pinched my cheek. "You a good boy. Have fun."

"Um, I'm not seven and going to a birthday party, but thanks."

I headed outside with a little spring in my stride. Stuart waved from the front seat and I waved back before I got in the car.

As soon as I got in, Stuart turned around. "This is going to be awesome," he said, like he was seven.

Stuart was funny that way. He could get excited about running in a gym or get excited about driving fast in a drug dealer's car without knowing the difference between the two events.

"You bet," I said. "I'm jacked to see you run."

We arrived at the soccer dome where the event was being held. They had decided to do it inside, just in case it rained or was cold. Spring had just sprung so the air could be winter or spring. Snow wasn't unusual at this time of year, but neither was a hot sunny day.

Upon entering, I went to the registration desk. Today's event was for Best Buddies clubs at different schools from all over the city and surrounding areas, so it wasn't just our Best Buddies group. Stuart and I signed in and were given t-shirts. He grinned like he'd been given a bike at Christmas.

"Wow! We get t-shirts! I'm putting it on right now." In front of everyone he whipped off his old t-shirt, exposing his skinny torso, and put on his new one. No shame there.

"It's so cool," he said, once he had it on.

I laughed. "It suits you." Suddenly, it hit me. I hadn't laughed, not really, in a long time.

I saw a group from our program and we headed over to them. Erika was dressed in shorts and her new t-shirt and what looked like new sneakers. As soon as she saw us she pointed to her feet.

"Look," she said. "New shoes."

Willa and Gloria were also there. Gloria's shoes were sort of cheap looking and worn, but she stuck out her feet, one after the other, like she was doing a dance.

"Mine are pink!" Gloria squealed.

Willa, put one of her feet in the middle too and said, "Mine are black high-tops!"

The group seemed excited to be at the event, but more excited about their t-shirts. Well, except Harrison, who wasn't going to wear his because he didn't wear new t-shirts that hadn't been washed and didn't have the tags removed.

The organizers called us all to the area where there was Astroturf and nets set up. They'd split the soccer pitches and made them into two, and it looked as if they were going to split the groups, but Buddies stayed with Buddies.

Once Stuart and I found out that we were on pitch four, I said, "I'll watch from the side, okay?" I was pretty nervous about running again, especially after chasing that car the other day. I didn't tell a soul about it either. Mention of that would have put my mother in heart failure, and one in a family is enough.

"Okay," said Stuart. He took off and ran to the middle of the field.

Although he was the only one out there without a Buddy, he ran around like a mad man, beating everyone to the soccer ball. And I mean everyone. His skills with kicking could have used some practice (well, a lot of practice) but, man, could he run.

As I watched, I noticed another boy who also had speed like Stuart. Every time Stuart went after the ball, the kid chased him hard. Stuart always got there first but the kid wasn't far behind.

I also noticed a girl on the field. She wasn't hard to notice because she was keeping everything organized, talking with this low gravelly voice, laughing like it came from the bottom of her stomach. She looked athletic, wearing her ball cap backwards, her long dark hair tucked behind her ears. Nothing went by her. She called out to the boys to pass the ball after they had chased it down. She joked and patted their backs and high-fived them if they did something even remotely good.

When the whistle blew for everyone to take a break, the girl went over to Stuart and the other fast kid and gave them both fist pumps. Then I saw Stuart point to me. They started to walk over.

I could tell she was Asian, but I couldn't pinpoint her nationality. Could be Korean or Thai or Vietnamese? Sweat ran down her face and glistened on her black hair. She wore plain black, knee-length satin basketball shorts and her event t-shirt. Now I was glad I'd gone to the can and put mine on too.

As she approached me, she pointed her thumb in Stuart's direction. "So, your guy is fast," she said in her raspy voice.

"Sure is," I said. "Great job, Stuart."

"I was fast," he said. "Bethany helped me." Stuart grinned at Bethany.

"He beat me every time," said the other boy. "And I'm in the Special Olympics."

The girl smiled at the boy, and I think he might have had FASD as well, but sometimes it's hard to tell. Some kids, like Stuart's brother Declan, sort of look like they might because some of them have a thin upper lip, but Stuart didn't have any of those physical characteristics.

"Dillon," she said to him, "you were great out there." She gave him a playful wink. "Good for you to have some competition."

"Both of you guys ripped it up," I said. I held up my hand and Stuart and Dillon high-fived it. Sweat trickled down Stuart's face.

"We should get some drinks and snacks," said this Bethany girl.

All four of us walked over to the table that had been set up with juice boxes and trays of fruit and granola bars. As the boys were picking up their drinks and pawing through the granola bars, I said to Bethany, "Thanks for helping Stuart."

"Hey, no problem. He really is a fast runner. I bet he could run track and field at school. He listened well."

"*Sometimes* he does," I said, playfully nudging Stuart. "You have your moments, right, Little Man?"

She laughed. "Sometimes I don't listen either, Stuart."

"Yeah, me too," I said.

Stuart and Dillon wandered over to Justin and Madeline, who were standing at the other end of the table. When they was out of earshot, Bethany said, "Honestly, you should look into the track club at your school for him. Dillon tried to go out for it at our school, but the coach didn't get him. He was kind of a hard nut. Made me so mad. Doesn't matter though because he's committed to Special Olympics and it's all his parents could handle anyway. Dillon does really well there. Last year, he won the 100 at the World Games."

"Wow," I said. "That's cool. I don't know much about the Special Olympics."

"Check it out online. It's pretty sweet."

"I will," I said. And I would. As soon as I got home.

I glanced at Bethany as she continued to talk. "They get Canadian track suits," she said, "and are treated like the real athletes that they are." She picked up a juice box and stuck the straw in.

"Who do they take for Special Olympics?" I didn't pick up a box because I hadn't run like the others.

She took a sip first before she said, "Oh, there are tons of kids. Anyone born with Down syndrome, Williams syndrome, fetal alcohol, cognitive issues from birth or even some sort of traumatic brain injury.

"You know a lot."

She grinned at me, and these really cute dimples stared me in the face. And her eyes. They were like lights almost. Bright and…honest. If that makes sense. When I realized I was staring, scorching heat hit my face.

"I'm one of the coaches," she said. "Well, as assistant as you can get." She smiled again. "You should come out one night. They do all kinds of sports."

Suddenly, it hit me that this was the first person I'd talked to that didn't know what had happened to me. I'd sheltered myself from people without really realizing I'd been doing it. Or did she know? I'd been plastered all over the newspapers and social media, and even television. Maybe she knew.

And just like that my mouth dried up. *Answer her. One way or the other.* I lowered my head, because I needed courage, and because I knew my face was red.

Say something.

"Um, sorry I didn't help out there." Not quite the comment I wanted to come out of my mouth, but at least I spoke.

"No problem," she said. "Stuart told me you had a heart problem."

"He did?" I immediately lifted my head and looked at her.

"Yeah. He was pretty detailed about it. And other things too." She glanced at me out of the corner of her eye, and again I noticed that cute grin, only this time she looked a little mischievous.

"Okay, spill. What else did he tell you?" I asked. Leave it to Stuart to go on about me. Sometimes he wouldn't talk and other times he talked non-stop. You never knew when the faucet would be turned on.

"For starters," she said, "you were the best basketball player on your team and the fastest runner and the captain. Oh, yeah, and your name was Sam. But really it was Samir because you were from somewhere far away."

"Um, I *was* born here," I said. "My parents are from Bosnia."

"Like me," she said. "Parents are from Vietnam, but I'm true blue Canadian." She snapped her fingers. "Oh yeah, he said you didn't have a girlfriend but you sort of did once but not for very long." Her lips were curled in amusement. "And Stuart was glad you didn't have *that* girlfriend anymore because *she* didn't like *him*."

Okay, although I was embarrassment personified, I still burst out laughing. Good ole Stuart with his lack of filter.

"He didn't leave much out," I said.

"Oh, I think he left a lot out." She wrinkled her nose and smiled at me.

CHAPTER ELEVEN
STUART

"I've got a great idea," Sam said to me at lunch on Monday.

I had a tuna sandwich and it smelled gross. "You want to buy me fries?" I grinned at Sam.

"No fries. I think you should join the track-and-field team for real."

I stared at him. "Me?"

"Yeah. I went to talk to the coach today and he said if I came with you and helped you, he would love to have you join the team."

I'd seen all the kids outside on those days when I went to see Donny. I wasn't supposed to see him anymore. I could go to jail. That's what Declan told me. My parents told me to stay away from him, and Declan said that if I hung out with him I would have to live in a cell and my toilet would be in there and if I had a dump I would have to smell it.

"Would you like to go to track and field?" Sam asked.

"You'd come with me?" I asked.

Sam nodded. "We could even try it today after school. I could phone your mom and she could pick you up at a later time. Or make some arrangements for someone to pick you up."

I flipped over a few more cards because I liked the game we were playing. "Sure," I said. "I've got two aces. Ha ha. I beat you."

Sam found me after school and told me I was going to track-and-field practice. I'd forgotten. That was okay. We walked down the hall together.

Now I was really going to track and field, and I was happy because I was going to get to run and maybe try those block things that the other kids use. I'd seen them on television because Andre De Grasse and Usain Bolt used them.

After I put on my gym clothes, I went outside with Sam and we walked over to the track. Before we got to the track, I saw a police car driving around by the recycling bins, going super slow. My parents said cops were going to monitor the school grounds. I hoped they wouldn't send me to jail. Declan said I might go to jail.

As we were walking over to the track, I saw Cecil. He was practising something called long jump where he ran as fast as he could, then jumped into a sand pit, and they measured how far he jumped with a measuring tape.

"Hey, dudes!" He gave Sam a playful punch on the shoulder. "Good to see ya out."

"Little Man here is going to see how he does at some of the running events," said Sam.

Cecil grinned at me and held up his hand and I smacked it hard. "That's fantabulous!" Then Cecil pointed to the track, and Sam and I turned around. The track coach waved at Sam.

"I better get him over there," he said to Cecil. Then he turned to me. "We better go."

"Run hard!" Cecil grinned at me and gave me a thumbs-up.

"I will," I said, and did the same thing.

As we walked away from Cecil, Sam asked me, "You know Mr. Rossi, right? He's the coach."

I didn't know Mr. Rossi, but I'd seen him in the hallways. I hoped he was nice and not a yelling kind of teacher. The yelling teachers always made me do things I didn't want to do.

"He runs most of the track events," said Sam, "and I think you'll do well at the 100 and 200—or maybe even 400."

I followed Stuart, but couldn't help staring at everyone. Stuff was going on everywhere, all over the place. Kids were high-jumping, and some were throwing the discus and shot put. I was staring so much I tripped over a bag.

"Focus," said Sam.

I nodded.

When we got to Mr. Rossi, he said, "Good to see you out, Stuart."

"Will I get to pop out of the blocks?" I asked. "Like Andre De Grasse or Usain Bolt."

"We are working on blocks today but how about we just get you running first, okay? I've got a bit of a program for you that I've given Sam. He can run you through it. You've started late and most of the other kids have been training for a few weeks already. The first school meet, to find qualifiers for the big city meet, is in a few weeks. You don't have a lot of time to train."

I didn't like that answer. "Why can't I work on the blocks?"

"I'll work with you on the blocks," said Sam quickly, "but just not today." He turned back to Mr. Rossi. "Would that be okay? I could maybe help him at lunch. Help him catch up."

"Let's just see how he does today," said Mr. Rossi. "I was going to run a few mock sprints, so let's have him join in."

Mr. Rossi handed Sam a piece of paper, then Sam had me walk over to the track but not where the other kids were practising on the blocks. I kept watching the other kids explode like rockets. That's what I wanted to do.

"First, you're going to run around the track once for warm-up," said Sam.

"That sounds boring," I said.

"Do you know how many boring things I had to do before I became a good basketball player?" Sam made a circle in the air with his finger. "Way you go. But not full speed, okay? It's just for warm-up."

"Okay." I took off running and although I really wanted to just run as fast as I could, I didn't. I did what Sam said. When I came around the corner of the track, I saw him waiting for me, so I started to run a little faster.

"Good," he said when I stopped in front of him. I wasn't breathing hard at all.

Next, he stretched with me and that was boring too, but I made it fun by picking little blades of grass. He made me hold the stretches, especially the ones that he said stretched the back of my legs and my thighs. He said the back of the legs were ham-somethings.

Then I had to jog on the spot with my knees high, which was stupid because I wasn't going anywhere. I kept watching the kids on the other side because they looked as if they were having way more fun than me.

"When are we going to do something fun?" I asked. I pointed over to the kids who were with Mr. Rossi. "Are we going to join them?"

"Yeah, soon," said Sam. "Mr. Rossi wants you to run against some of the other runners just to see where you're at. You get to race today! Let's just finish warming up alone."

"Okay," I said. "I get to race?"

"Sure do. But only if you keep warming up."

We did a few more things, like jump squats and something else that he called a mountain climb, but we weren't climbing any mountain that I could see. I sort of wished I was with Donny instead of at track because I got to play video games with him. Finally, Sam said we could go over to the other runners.

When we got over to where they were, Mr. Rossi called everyone in. I was the smallest and skinniest.

"We're going to do a few sprints," he said. "First the 100, then the 200. Just for some simulation practice for the upcoming school meet."

"Can we use the blocks?" a boy asked.

Mr. Rossi looked at me and kind of squinted as if he was thinking. Then he said to everyone, "Since we just started to practise with them, how many of you want to try?"

Everyone put up their hand but me and another boy. So I put up my hand too.

"Okay. Why not?" Mr. Rossi pulled his clipboard out from under his arm. "Most of you can try. Stuart," he looked right at me, "since you didn't work with them today, I want you to race without them."

"Um, that's not totally fair to Stuart," said Sam. "That others get to use blocks."

"It's not our fault he's shown up late," muttered the boy beside me.

I heard someone else mumble, "As if blocks would help *him*."

"You shoulda let me use the blocks," I said to Sam.

"*Shhh*," he said.

"I'll take that into consideration when looking at the times," said Mr. Rossi.

Mr. Rossi gave us all a number and that number was our lane. There were enough kids in our age group to do three heats. We weren't going against the older kids because we were called the "juniors." I'm not very good at math so I had no idea how many were running, but I remembered that I was number six, so I should go to lane six, and Sam told me I was in the first heat.

As Sam walked me over to lane six, he asked me, "Do you know what a heat is?"

I shrugged.

"You are going to race against the first group of runners. Only three from your race will move on and race the final race. Do you understand?"

I shrugged again. "I have lane six."

"That's great you know that," he said. "Okay, so just run as fast as you can in this first race. If you come in the top three, you will get to race again."

I grinned. "Twice. That's cool." Maybe this could be fun.

"For sure. Just go as fast as Andre De Grasse."

"He's kind of small too."

"And stay in your lane, okay? Run straight. And listen for Mr. Rossi to say *Go* before you take off. He'll say, 'On your marks, set, GO.' You go on GO, okay?"

I nodded. I lined up in lane six. Suddenly, I felt all jittery because I was so excited. I stared straight ahead and saw the white lines. I'd watched the Olympics on television, so I knew how to run straight. I wasn't sure how to start but I crouched a little. Sam was still with me.

"Is this good?" I asked.

"For today, sure," said Sam. "Put one leg in front and one leg behind. And push off the back foot. Go low first then get to standing."

I stood up because crouching was hurting my legs. But then Mr. Rossi started talking and Sam whispered, "Get back in your crouch. Wait for the word *GO.*"

Sam walked away. The guy beside me crouched because he was the only one who said he didn't want to use blocks. So, I did what he did. Stood with one leg forward and the other leg back and my arms ready to pump.

Mr. Rossi said, "On your marks."

I stared straight ahead.

Then he said, "Set!"

The white lines went all the way down the track.

"GO!"

I took off! Running. Running. Down the track as fast as I could go.

At first, I was behind the boy beside me but I wanted to catch him, so I pumped harder and harder and I started to go by him. Faster. Faster. Faster. I crossed the line, but I couldn't just stop running. My legs were like a car trying to slow down without using the brakes. Finally, I slowed down and I had to catch my breath. I'd never run *that* fast before. I panted, breathing in and out. I'd never had to breathe like this before, after running.

Sam came over to me and patted my back.

"That was amazing!" He started to laugh, like he was kind of crazy. "You were incredible."

"Did I win?" I asked.

"You sure did! You killed it. I can't believe it." He glanced down the track toward the start line. "The next group is getting set up. Let's get off the track and walk you out. You'll be running again soon because you made it through to the next heat!"

I looked at Sam and saw this big smile on his face, just like when he won a basketball game. "You're happy," I said.

He tilted his head when he looked back at me. "Yeah," he said. "Funnily enough, I am. Come on, we've got to get you ready."

We walked around and he told me to keep shaking out my legs, and he also made me stretch. When we heard Mr. Rossi yelling *GO*, we stopped to watch the other runners. I saw a boy running who didn't like me very much (once he stuck out his foot and tripped me when I was running in the hallway), and he came third. Sam told me he would be in my next race.

"I don't want to stand by him," I said.

"Why not?"

"He doesn't like me."

"That's okay," said Sam. "Who cares?" He leaned in to me and whispered, "I bet you can beat him."

"What if he trips me?"

"I'll make sure he doesn't."

We watched for a little longer and then Sam's phone rang. He pulled it out of his pocket and looked at the number.

"Is it my mom?" I asked.

"No. It's Bethany. Do you remember her from the I Can Play event?"

I tried to think back to that day.

"She was with the boy who ran fast like you," he said.

"Is she your girlfriend now?"

"No."

"Are you kissy-facing with her, like that cheerleader girl does with Smitty from your basketball team? He got so mad at me the other day and told me to stop staring at them kissing even though I wasn't."

"No, I'm not," he said. "But…I wish." He kind of muttered that last part but I still heard him. The phone stopped ringing.

"How come you didn't talk to her?" I pointed to his phone.

"I'm with you right now. I'll talk to her later," he said. "How about if I send her a text and tell her you're running. She'll understand." He sent the text then put his phone back in his pocket.

I liked that. It made me feel good inside that he was my friend again. I reached out and hugged him and he patted my back, but then he pulled away.

"We need to get you focused again." Sam looked away from me and at something on the other side of the track.

Was it Donny? He wasn't supposed to come around because the cops were cruising. I didn't want to go to jail. I turned to see what Sam was looking at and I saw Cecil walking toward us, looking like he was finished his long jumping already.

When Cecil got closer he raised his hand high in the air. I jumped to smack it.

"Way to go, Little Man. You cleaned up."

"He's got another race to do," said Sam.

"They doing 200 too?"

"Think so," said Sam. "But first they're doing the 100 again. He's made it to the next round." Sam held up his thumbs like he was super excited for me.

"How come you're not running this year?" I asked Cecil. He ran last year and won a medal.

"I'm focusing one hundred percent on b-ball, dude. Just gonna do the long jump for fun and 'cause Mr. Rossi asked me to. Good for points for the school. He wants to win the city trophy this year." Cecil grinned at me. "How many events you going in, Little Man?"

"I dunno."

"I'm thinking he'll clean up in 400 too," said Sam.

"How far is that?" I asked.

"Once around the track," said Sam. "You might be a natural because you can run forever."

"Will I do that one today too?" I asked. I started counting all these races on my fingers. Sounded like a lot.

"Maybe. Just focus on one race at a time." Sam waved to someone across the field, then he said, "Mr. Rossi is calling us over now."

"I'll watch," said Cecil. "Go fast, Little Man."

Sam and I walked over to where Mr. Rossi stood with his clipboard.

"Stuart," he said, "you're in lane six again."

I nodded. Sam said thanks to Mr. Rossi and we walked to the start line again.

"Just do what you did last time," said Sam.

"As soon as he says GO, I run in a straight line."

"That's it, that's all," said Sam.

The boy who tripped me in the hallway was in lane 5 and I didn't want to be beside him. "I don't want this lane," I said.

Sam leaned into me to talk to me. "I specifically asked Mr. Rossi for the same lane as last time to make it easier for you," whispered Sam.

"I don't want him to trip me." I jerked my head to the boy beside me.

"Don't worry, he won't." Sam leaned in again and whispered. "Just focus on running."

"I don't want to run beside him," I said loudly.

This time Sam took my shoulders and moved me away from the boy. "I'm going to give you two choices," he said. "Run with him beside you. Or don't run at all. And if you don't run, you won't be able to win. What do you want to do?"

I was always supposed to pick. *Choose*. I did want to run because I did want to win again.

"I'll run beside him," I said.

When Sam was leaving I heard him talk to the boy beside me. "Don't even think about it," he said to him.

Again, I lined up and tried to do that crouch thing that helped me last time. When Mr. Rossi yelled *GO*, I took off again, running, arms pumping, legs striding forward. I passed the guy who tripped me but not the guy on my other side. He kept pushing harder and harder and I kept trying to catch him, but I just couldn't get him and then we crossed the finish line.

This time my legs were shaking. I thought I might collapse on the track but instead I bent over, and everything was all blurry for a second. I felt a hand on my back and I stood. Sam was beside me and Cecil had come over too.

"How'd I do?" I asked.

"Third!" Sam sounded excited even though I didn't win. "You've hardly practised. I mean, you're raw, so that's amazing."

"You were a lightning bolt," said Cecil.

"I didn't win," I said.

"Hey, this is your first go around out here," said Sam. "You didn't even use blocks."

"Are we going to, one day?" I asked.

"Of course."

"During math class we can practise."

Cecil burst out laughing. "I like your attitude."

The next race I had to do was the 200 and Sam explained how I couldn't leave my lane and how I had to run halfway around the track.

I lined up and went on the word *GO*. I kind of liked the curve as it made me feel as if I was in a race car going around a corner and using a steering wheel. I didn't run beside the boy who tripped me, but I ran fast again and I crossed the line in second place.

Mr. Rossi only made us do that one once and he said he would compare all our times because parents were coming to pick up kids and there wasn't enough time.

"Great job, again," said Sam. He held up his hand for a high-five. Usually, I high-fived him after basketball but now *he* was high-fiving me.

"How are you feeling?" Sam asked me.

"Good."

"Would you like to run once around the track as fast as you can? Mr. Rossi wants to get a ballpark time for you for the 400 metre. I know you've done a lot today, but you're nailing it. Are you okay to do one more?"

"I guess so."

"Are you tired?"

"I can run once around." I saw all the parents and wondered where my mom was. "When is my mom coming?"

"Soon," he said. "If she comes in time, she can watch you."

"Okay," I said.

Mr. Rossi had me line up kind of where the 100 ends, like in the middle of the track. "So, just go once around," he said. "As fast as you can."

"I can go fast?"

He smiled at me. "Yes, you can. So far you've gone really fast. I've been impressed. Give it everything you've got."

I lined up, got in my crouch, and when he said *GO*, I took off and ran.

After running around the first bend, I got really tired and had to slow down a little. This was hard because no one was running with me. My heart beat really fast. And my legs felt like they were on fire.

I looked forward. I was running straight now, and I went past the halfway mark or what I thought was halfway. My legs were still burning. I had to keep running. That's what I was supposed to do.

Now, the next bend was close. So close. One more bend and then I could run straight again. I rounded it. Pretended I was steering a car around it. Going fast. Air flying through my hair.

Then I had a straightaway. I could see Sam at the finish line. And my mom and Declan and Mary! I tried to take longer strides and increase how fast I was going.

"Go, Stuart, go!" Sam yelled. That made me go even faster.

"Go, Stuart!" My mom yelled too. And so did Declan and Mary.

I crossed the finish line and slowed down. My heart was beating like a machine gun going off. *Boom. Boom. Boom.* Over and over.

My mom came over to me and walked with me.

"Stuart, that was wonderful," she said.

"My heart is beating like an automatic machine gun and feels like it's going to send a bullet right out of my shirt," I said.

"That's because you ran so fast," she said. "Randy said you would do well at this, but I didn't know how well."

Mr. Rossi came over to me and said, "That was really good, Stuart. With a little training you could have a decent 400 time. I'm pleased."

"Really?"

"Really." He smiled at me. "See you tomorrow after school."

"Oh, he'll be here," said my mother. Then she turned to Sam. "That is if Sam is willing to help him."

"I'm on it," he said.

CHAPTER TWELVE
SAM

"He's a natural." I pointed to the track. Stuart's mother had come to pick him up and had brought Declan and Mary.

"He's halfway through the 400 right now," I said. I took a quick glance at my phone where I was timing him. "I've got him at a great pace." Mr. Rossi was also timing him and that would be the official time.

"Wow," said Mary, as she watched him. "I'm impressed. Look at him go." Mary was obviously pregnant. She looked huge.

"How come he's running by himself?" Declan asked.

"He's running for time," I said, keeping my eyes on Stuart as he ran through the halfway mark, heading toward the last bend. "Here he comes around the last corner!"

"Go, Stuart!" his mother yelled. Mary joined in and so did Declan. Soon they were all yelling for Stuart and he grinned (not sure how he could when he was running full tilt) as he crossed the finish line.

Mr. Rossi snapped his stopwatch, and I took my phone over to compare times.

Stuart now walked with his hands on his hips, head down, trying to catch his breath. His family surrounded him, telling him how great he had done. I watched him and something inside me expanded, like my heart was going to burst out of my skin. He'd worked hard, like really hard. Harder than I ever imagined he would or even could.

Mr. Rossi nodded at me as he showed me the time on the watch. "Not bad," he said. "Not bad at all. He's never practised and he had to run the other races at full tilt before running this. I'm impressed. One minute, five seconds. I bet he could get that time down to a minute flat if he trained and tapered. That would be pretty incredible for someone his age and size."

"Wow, that is fast," I said. "When I was his age, I was never below 60 seconds."

Stuart's mother came over to Mr. Rossi.

"Hello," she said, holding out her hand. "I'm Stuart's mother and I want to thank you so much for allowing Stuart to be part of the program."

"I'm happy he's here." Mr. Rossi shook her hand. "He did well today."

"I'm so glad to hear that," she said.

"I think he's going to be an asset to our school team," said Mr. Rossi. Then he glanced at me. "Sam has agreed to be with him, so that will keep him focused."

He gestured for Stuart (who was still with Declan and Mary) to come over.

All three of them walked over to us. Mr. Rossi patted Stuart's shoulder. "Make sure you have a hot bath tonight. You ran a lot today."

"I run a lot every day."

"Maybe that's why you're fast," said Mr. Rossi with a smile. "Wish all my runners were like you. Make sure you stretch too."

"I can help him stretch," said Declan. "I read all kinds of fitness magazines."

"Sam stretches me," said Stuart. He held up his hand and I high-fived it.

"Declan can help you at home, Little Man," I said.

"Mary can't," said Stuart. "Her stomach is way too big to even bend over. She's having a baby."

"I can see that," said Mr. Rossi with a little grin. He turned to her and said, "Congratulations."

"We should get going," said Stuart's mother. "Let Mr. Rossi go home."

I helped Stuart gather his things and then we all walked to his mother's car.

"Why did you *all* come?" he asked his family.

"We were out shopping to buy a few things for the baby," said his mother. "And Declan needed a new pair of pants for work, so he tagged along."

"For work? You got a job?" Stuart asked Declan. "Like a real job?"

"I'm going to work at Best Buy every Saturday," Declan said with pride in his voice.

"Best Buy!" exclaimed Stuart. "You'll be surrounded by video games all day. I want a job. Maybe I can work there too."

"Stuart, I think this track and field will be enough for now," said his mother, putting her arm around him. "Maybe when you're older. Let's just focus on one thing, okay?"

"Okay. If I run in a real meet, will you come watch?"

"Of course!" His mother squeezed his shoulder. "All of us."

When we got to their car, I said goodbye and gave Stuart yet another huge high-five. That had to be…how many this afternoon? His mother in turn thanked me over and over, which got a bit embarrassing. I hadn't really done *that* much. Stuart was the one who ran.

As I walked home, I pulled my phone out of my pocket, wanting to tell someone about what had gone down at the track-and-field practice. I thought about sending something to Elma but, crap, she was my sister. Lame or what?

There was one person who I really wanted to tell. Bethany and I had exchanged numbers at the I Can Play event so that she could share the information on the Special Olympics practices with me. We *had* texted about that. But that's it, that's all.

Should I text her about this? Could I? She would understand how amazing the afternoon had been. Sure, Cecil was there and thought it was cool, and Stuart's family had shown up. But I wanted to tell *her* because it had been her idea.

I kept walking, tossing my phone from one hand to the next. A text would be nothing really. Just a text. About Stuart. More walking. More talking to myself. I wished I had a photo to send of Stuart. But I didn't take any. I'd been too immersed in his practice to take photos.

More walking. *Come on, just send a text.*

Finally, I got up the nerve.

Stuart had a great track and field practice thx for suggestion

I pressed send then stuffed my phone in my jacket. I hadn't taken more than five steps when my phone pinged. With fumbling hands, I yanked it out of my pocket, almost dropping it. I stopped to read the text.

that's so amazing

Thumbs flying, I typed: *coach wants him to run in school meet*

Wow when

soon end of next week

cool you should come to Special Olympics this week check out the track and field

might be too much for him? maybe just I should come

Good excuse to see her again. I waited for her answer.

Perfect. just you come he can come after his meet

I breathed a sigh of relief. She wanted me to come. Me! I hurried to send the next message.

k when where

She gave me the details (Friday night at the university indoor track) and I was about to pop my phone back in my pocket when I heard bike brakes screeching behind me.

"Yo, dude. You're in la-la-land." Cecil circled me on his bike, wearing a stupid grin on his face. "Who ya texting that you can't walk at the same time?

I shoved my phone in a pocket and started walking. "My mom."

"Seriously? Your mama makes you smile like that?" He popped his bike up, doing a wheelie. "I don't believe you." The bike popped back down, and he hopped off without missing a beat.

I shrugged. "It's not like I'm popular these days."

We walked in silence for a few steps, his bike sounding as if the chain could use some oiling. Finally, he spoke. "Hey, what you did for Little Man today was cool."

"Two-way street, bro."

For the next two days, I met up with Stuart after school and we headed out to the track to practise. I had made up programs which I discussed with Mr. Rossi, and together we tweaked what Stuart needed to do. Online programs helped me create his workouts. Stuart liked some of the stuff we did but not all of it, that was for sure. His attention span was limited.

"You said we could work with the blocks," he said on Thursday. He crossed his arms across his chest and scowled at me. "I'm not practising today unless we do the blocks." He planted his feet and held his stance. There was no way he was going to budge. I knew that look.

"Mr. Rossi doesn't think you need blocks."

Rossi wanted us to work on his fitness for a bit more before introducing the blocks. He even suggested that we might ditch the blocks altogether for the school meet and have him run without since he had joined late.

"You said I could try them. I don't want to do boring stuff again."

"Okay, okay," I said. There was a part of me that was worried I wasn't making the practices fun enough. He loved the racing but not the repetitive stuff.

"I'll see what I can do," I said. "Let's go talk to Mr. Rossi."

"I have to pee," he said.

"Okay. Go ahead. Meet me out at the track."

He nodded and turned to head back into the school.

I hustled out to the track, as in jogged, sort of. I talked to Mr. Rossi and explained the situation. He agreed but suggested we work alone, somewhere quiet to keep Stuart's focus.

About five minutes after talking to Mr. Rossi, I started to get worried. Where was Stuart? Had he left? Had he forgotten where we were to meet? Crap. I scanned the field, thinking maybe he'd stopped to talk to Cecil. But I couldn't see him. I headed to the back doors of the school, the ones we'd come out of, but he wasn't on his way back. My heart started thumping. Sweat popped out on my brow. Restroom. Maybe he was still sitting on the can. I rushed inside and checked the closest restroom, calling his name. No answer. No feet under the stalls either.

I hustled back outside. *Where was he?* I called his name. Once. Twice. Third time was like a loud croak. My heart sped up and was now hammering inside me. My stomach felt sick. I called out again.

My throat felt as if it was closing in on me. I almost couldn't breathe. How could he disappear so quickly? I'd only been gone seven, eight minutes, max.

I was about to turn around and head to the track area when I heard a familiar sound. That car! Coming from the street at the side of the school. I turned to see the blue car inching down the street away from the school. Where were the cops? I scanned the streets. Gone. Probably left just after three, when school ended. Had Stuart gone with him again?

Suddenly, Stuart appeared from around a big clump of shrubs, walking toward me.

"Where were you?" I asked, shaking from head to toe.

"I had to pee," he said.

"You should have gone in the school." My voice wobbled.

"Too far," he said. "I wanted to go behind that shrub."

"Was that *Donatello's* car I heard?

"I don't know no Donatello," he said.

"Okay, Donny."

"I dunno." He shrugged.

Did he hear the car? Did he not hear the car? I didn't want to push this or scare him or…send him running away, instead of running with the track team. I stared at him as he looked at his shoe and kicked the dirt. Was he lying to me?

"Wasn't Donny," he said. Stuart wouldn't make eye contact with me.

Okay. He *was* lying. "Little Man," I said. "Stay away from him. He could get you in a lot of trouble." I paused for a second. "Look at me," I said. When he did, I pointed to the track. "Mr. Rossi says it's okay for you to use the blocks. Want to get started?"

"Okay." His face lit up.

We walked back to the track and I picked up a set of blocks. Then I moved us to a quiet area. My hands were still shaking when I set the blocks up on the grass. After I showed him what to do, he practised over and over. He liked doing it too; this repetition was something he could focus on. He would burst out like a madman. His excitement calmed me down.

After around fifteen minutes, I said, "We should go check in with Mr. Rossi."

"Can I show him how good I am?"

"Sure," I said.

As we walked out to the track area, I kept searching for Dunn's car but it was gone. Stuart's parents needed to know about this. Out on the track, the runners were doing a fast-run/slow-run drill around the track.

"Can I do that?" Stuart asked.

"I don't see why not." Personally, I thought he should integrate with the other runners. After all, the school meet was only a week away. I talked to Mr. Rossi on Stuart's behalf and he was okay with him giving it a whirl. I took Stuart aside and talked to him.

"You have to listen for the whistle," I said. "When it blows, you run as fast as you can. When it blows again, you walk. You might go around the track a few times with this drill."

He nodded. "Okay."

He set up with the other kids and I watched closely to make sure no one was tripping him or talking down to him. I also watched that he listened. And he did. When the exercise ended, he came over to me.

"That was more fun than stretching," he said.

"You did great."

"I passed some kids," he said.

"Lots of them."

Mr. Rossi blew his whistle and called everyone in. I stood with Stuart who stood behind the group, barely able to see over everyone's heads. All the time that I had played sports, I had stood in the front of the pack to show the coach I was keen. Even though Stuart was the smallest kid in the group, he hung back, like that was his place. It was all I could do not to push him forward, but I didn't want to make a scene.

Mr. Rossi talked about the school meet, and how he would put up a sign-up sheet and how each runner got to pick up to three events. I already knew that Stuart would be able to handle the 100, 200, and 400. We would look for the sign-up sheet together, but he needed to fill in his name for himself, so it would give him a sense of ownership. Like, this was *his* thing.

I made sure I walked Stuart to the front of the school and waited with him until his mother came to pick him up. I kept looking up and down the street for any sight of Dunn, but he didn't reappear. I didn't want to alert Stuart's mother in front of him.

Stuart pointed to his mother's car, which had just pulled up. "There's my mom."

"Great work, today," I said. "Remember, no practice tomorrow. It's Friday. And we'll sign you up for three events tomorrow morning when the sheet goes up. I'll text your mom and get her to drop you off early so we can do that."

He nodded. Then we did our usual high-five and he took off for his mother's car. He was safe. I don't know why I felt like a weight was lifted, but I did.

Later that night I sent a message to Stuart's mother about no practice Friday, early sign-up, and times for next week. And about Dunn nosing around. She immediately texted me back, thanking me for the heads up.

The next morning, Stuart and I met, and he signed himself up for the 100, 200, and 400 metre races. I watched as he signed his own name, and this time I took a photo. Once I'd sent it to his mother, I also sent it to Bethany. She responded with a happy face that made me grin. The rest of the day became a bit of a blur for me as I had a big test in math and a group presentation in social. Lunch was a meeting with the group, so I didn't get to see Stuart again.

By the time the 3:00 bell let us out for the weekend, I was glad to get out of there. Plus, for the first time since I'd been out of the hospital, I had something to do on a Friday night that I was looking forward to.

Since the Special Olympics deal didn't start until 7:00 p.m., I sat down for dinner with my parents. Lately, Elma hadn't been around as much. I guess she'd gone back to having a life instead of playing the part of my personal nurse and checking up on me. Mom had made lamb and beef kebobs, which she served with pita bread, sour cream, and ajvar.

At dinner, we often talked Bosnian if Elma was around. Since Elma wasn't having dinner with us tonight, I tried to steer the conversation to English.

"Good dinner, Mom."

"Glad you like. Tonight you go out?" she asked.

I spooned some ajvar on pita. "Yup."

My mother frowned at me. "You say 'yup'. That not English."

"Yes, Mother. I. Am. Going. Out. Tonight. Is that better?" I slid the meat off the kebab and rolled up the pita.

"You being what is called a smart-aleck," said my father. He bit into his pita.

"Sorry," I said. Before I took a bite, I said, "I'm going out to a Special Olympics practice that they have in the city. I want to see if it would be something Stuart would like."

"Nice," said my mother. "How you hear about this?"

I pointed to my mouth. Chewing hunks of lamb could take a few seconds. Finally, I wiped my mouth with my paper serviette.

"I met a few people at the I Can Play event who work with some of the athletes. Might be okay to get involved." I shrugged. "I'll see tonight."

"Good," said my mother. "Tell about this Special Olympics."

I started spewing off information. "It's for people with intellectual disabilities. Like the kids in the Best Buddies group. They do all kinds of sports like track and field, basketball, badminton and even skating and skiing in the winter. Oh, and they do bocce, Dad."

"Bocce!"

I knew my dad had played a lot of bocce when he was in Bosnia.

"To je dobar sport," said my dad in Bosnian.

"Yeah, it's your kind of sport," I said, laughing.

"This good for you," said my mother. "Helping is good. In camp I teach children reading."

"I didn't know you did that," I said. Actually, I didn't know a lot of what had happened. Some. But obviously not everything. Elma talked a little about what it was like, eating rice day in and day out, and maybe having a little chicken and that would be a treat. It was weird for me to think my family had been in the camp, lived that sparse life for five years, without me even being born yet. Almost as if we were two separate families.

I had been told that when they were able to return to Bosnia, they lost their home because it was occupied, even though they owned it. They showed up at the front door and people were living in it and wouldn't leave. That's why they took such pride in our Canadian house.

Now it was my father's turn to wipe the red ajvar and dripping sour cream off his mouth. Kebabs were messy. He put his serviette down and said, "Your mother a good teacher."

"And you good at selling things," said my mother.

My father waved his hand in front of his face.

To make extra money for the family, my dad had sold "stuff" at flea markets. Elma told me she used to love going along with him when she was little and playing dress-up with some of the clothes he sold.

"That's a good skill to have, Dad."

"Yah, yah," he said, waving his hand in front of his face. "Not for me."

We finished eating and I helped my mother with the dishes before I got my coat on to leave.

"You need ride?" my father asked.

"I'm okay. I can catch the bus."

"I drive," he said. He winked at me. "I want ice cream."

We got in the car and I plugged the address into my phone. We didn't talk a lot on the drive, but then my dad and I didn't actually talk a lot in general. Elma called him the "man of few words." It's just who he was.

"You have bucks for tonight?" he asked.

My dad had these slang words he had picked up when he arrived in Canada and they had stuck with him over the years. *Bucks* for *money* was one of them. "I've got a little," I said.

More silence. But it was comfortable. He pulled up outside the door to the sports arena.

Bethany stood by the doors, as if she was waiting for me. As soon as she saw us drive up, she waved.

"*Ko je ta devojka?*" My father peered out the window and I wanted to sink in the seat and slither out the back door. No go. He'd seen her now, and asked who she was.

"Um, *Rekla mi je o programa.*" I had to tell him something and I made it easy by just saying she told me about the program.

"I won't tell Mother," he said, back to broken English. Then he gave me this weird fatherly slap on the back and a grin that made me almost roll my eyes. It was as if he was happy to be a part of some big secret.

"Appreciate that," I said. "And don't tell Elma either."

"*Ne Elma,*" he said, laughing.

I got out of the car, shut the door, and waited for him to drive away. When it was obvious he wasn't leaving ASAP, I headed over to Bethany.

"Hi," I said.

"I'm so glad you came." The corners of her mouth turned up and she glanced over at my father in the car that still hadn't moved. "Um, is that your dad?"

"Yeah. Let's move inside. He'll leave then."

I held the door open for her or else I would have gotten a lecture about manners when I got home. Once inside I finally exhaled.

"I'm so glad you came," she said. As she walked, I swear she bounced on her toes. She wasn't tall, but she was definitely compact. Her hair was up in a ponytail and it swung back and forth. "You're going to love the athletes."

"I like that you call them athletes," I said.

"Because they are. Wait until you see what they can do. How's Stuart, by the way?"

"He's doing great. Next week is our school meet. On Thursday. Today we put his name down to be in three events, so he should stay busy."

"Our program winds down a bit in the summer, unless the athletes are competing at a championship. Maybe you can get him out here once the school meet is over. It's a little more forgiving here, mostly in practice, but there are rules as well. Many are the same."

We walked down a few halls, then through a door, and suddenly I was in the indoor track and there were kids doing all kinds of activities; sprinting at one end of the track, hurdle running on the other. High-jumping in one corner. Even weight-lifting in another corner.

"Wow," I said. "I thought you said tonight was just track and field."

She laughed. "Oh, that's Ben. He lifts all the time so we just give him a little space to work. He's a champion—wins all kinds of medals."

"Incredible," I said.

"Yeah, it's pretty cool." She nodded her head.

The hour flew by and I mainly just hung out with Bethany, almost like her shadow, and watched her coach the runners through starts. She was firm, funny, and...they loved her.

Some used the blocks and others didn't. It was up to each athlete to decide. From watching, I knew that Stuart would be as good as any of them with his natural stride and endurance.

At the end of the time, I helped put the equipment and mats away.

"So, what'd you think?" Bethany asked.

"This would be great for Stuart. How did you get to be a coach?" I asked.

"You have to take a course and there are levels to go through, just like any coaching certification. It's not hard, just time consuming. It's a few weekends here and there." She smiled and her eyes shone. For some reason my face heated up. I had to look away.

All night I'd been thinking about how I could ask her to go to a coffee shop with me after this was all over. It was only 8:30. We could go for an hour. Talk. But I felt like my tongue was swollen even though I'd already googled coffee shops on campus and found one open.

"Um," I started. That's as far as I got before one of Bethany's athletes, a girl named Dawn, came up and wrapped her arms around her waist. "That was fun," she said. She had been born with Down syndrome. Bethany hugged her back.

"You did great tonight, Dawn," said Bethany. "I loved how you worked as hard as you could." Then she pulled away and looked over at me. "Did you meet my friend?"

Dawn looked up at me. She probably was only four feet tall. "Is he your boyfriend?" she asked.

Bethany's face instantly turned red. Mine too. In fact, this time my flush travelled from my neck, to my face, to the ends of my ear lobes. My whole head felt as if it had been stuck in a hot oven to bake. I tried to duck and just casually look around.

"He's my friend," said Bethany, speaking for both of us. Bethany looked into the distance and pointed. "Your sister is here to pick you up."

After Dawn left with her sister, Bethany said, "Well, that was awkward."

I laughed. "Sure was." It was now or never. "You, um, want to go for coffee somewhere?" There! I'd got it out. Now I waited. *Please say yes.*

She looked at me, all calm and casual, and smiled. "Sounds good to me."

We found the coffee shop, after a few wrong turns. It was a place where, after coffee hours, musicians played. Tonight there was a girl with long hair playing her guitar and singing some Adele song. We found a table and I ordered a Coke and Bethany ordered a fruit drink.

At first, we didn't say much of anything beyond commenting on our drinks and I was starting to feel as if things were going horribly and that I sucked at doing this kind of thing because, well, I'd never really done it before. Girls had always just come to me and we hung out at school for awhile, then hung out at parties, then at our houses, and eventually we just became an item. And really, there had only been Traci and Rachel, and both of them had lasted all of a month each. Sports had been my focus.

This seemed so different, sitting in a coffee shop, talking about something besides our school, and our school basketball team, and so-and-so, and so on.

"So," she said, leaning back in her chair. "What's your favourite movie?"

In all my time at home, moping around, I'd read about this game in one of Elma's magazines. It was supposedly a good way to get to know your "date." I think the magazine had been *Cosmopolitan*. But this wasn't really a "date." I was pretty sure I wasn't going in for the first kiss. Although, right now, looking at her across from me, I'd like that to happen. This girl was different, and instead of being the typically "hot" one, she had spunk and energy, which I really, really liked.

I forced myself to think about the question. I had a ton of favourite movies. Mostly funny ones like *Wedding Crashers* and *40-Year-Old Virgin* and *Yes, Man*. But then I thought of another one I'd watched with Elma and my parents because my dad loved it, and it left me thinking. Maybe it would impress her.

"It's a really old one," I finally said, "but *The Green Mile*."

"I've never heard of that one," she said.

Okay, so I'd bombed. Tried to be too intellectual or something. "I think you'd like it," I said quickly. "It's a Stephen King movie, but it's a drama, not a horror movie." Then I asked, "What's yours?"

She grinned. "I'm going to sound super shallow but *Wedding Crashers*." She laughed. "It is hilarious. I also loved *Bridesmaids*. I've watched it so many times."

I slapped my forehead. "I was going to say *Wedding Crashers*," I said.

"Well, you didn't. And I did." She gave me a playful little smirk, and tilted her head. "I have another question."

"Shoot," I said. I figured she was going to ask me about my favourite food and I was ready to say pizza.

But she said, "Tell me about your family, Mr. Sokolovic. Oh, and by the way, if you don't know, my last name is Phong." This time she grinned. "It's always good to know a girl's last name."

CHAPTER THIRTEEN
STUART

I didn't want to see Donny again, but I did anyway. It wasn't my fault though. I didn't mean to see him. It was our last practice on Thursday, before the weekend, and Sam told me we were a week away from the school track-and-field meet. I wanted to work with the blocks. Every practice he said we could but then we didn't.

Finally, we were going to. But I had to pee first. I'd found some money on the kitchen counter this morning so I'd had two sodas for lunch. The restroom was like a mile away, inside the school, and I had to go real bad.

I looked up and saw a whole whack of bushes and they already had leaves. The bushes were as good a place as any because no one was here to tell me they weren't. I ran behind them, looked around, and when I didn't see anyone, I peed.

I was down to a dribble when I heard the car. I knew the sound. I wasn't supposed to see Donny. Never. Ever. Again. Or I would go to jail. I tried to hurry my pee and zip up my pants.

"Stu," he called out to me.

I turned and saw him coming toward me. He had a video game in his hand. "I've been looking for you," he said. He moved toward me. "I wanted you to have this."

He handed me the video game, the one I had played at his house. *Kill Zone*. I loved that game. "You're giving it to me?"

"Sure am, Stu. Don't tell anyone though." He winked at me. "We have good secrets. Right? You didn't tell anyone about me? Did you?"

I looked down at the box and my body got jittery. "No," I said.

"Good going. It wouldn't be good for either of us if you did."

"I didn't say anything."

"I hope not."

"I won't tell about the video game either."

"Good boy. Maybe you can come over again one day. Or ride in my car."

I wanted to go fast in his car again. But I didn't want to go to jail.

Suddenly, I heard Sam calling my name as if he was looking for me. It's what my mother sounded like when I used to run away from her in the mall, when I was little.. His voice sounded kind of high.

"You better go," said Donny. "Run."

"I'm on the track-and-field team," I said.

"I know. I like that you're running fast. Handy skill, kid."

"You do?"

"Oh, yeah. That speed, kid—it's a good thing in my business." He started walking away from me, but he was walking backwards.

"Oh, and hide that thing in the bushes," he said, pointing to the game in my hands. "You can come back and get it later. Remember, it's yours and only yours. Don't show anyone or they will take it away from you." Then he took off to his car.

Sam wasn't calling me anymore, so I stashed the video just like Donny said. Way back under the bush. Then I heard Sam again, so I walked out from behind the bush.

Sam didn't seem to be too mad at me for going pee in the bushes, and actually looked happy to see me. I sure didn't tell him about Donny.

"Let's work with the blocks," said Sam. His voice sounded so weird.

Sam showed me what to do and I practised with them, doing what he said to do, which was really fun. Then I got to run with the other kids.

As I was running around, stopping and starting when the whistle blew, one of the kids told me I sucked. So, I ran by him and told him to "take that and shove it." He said he was going to get me good. I kept running and beat him.

On Saturday, I had to go shopping with my father because he wanted to buy me new running shoes to wear for my races. Something lighter to make me faster. There were so many running shoes to pick from but the guy who was helping me try them knew which ones would be good for me. Out of the colours I got to pick from were yellow and blue, and orange and blue, and black and red. I picked the red and black pair.

Then when we got home I told my dad I was going for a run at the school track to try out my new shoes. My dad said he would drive me over and even run with me.

When we were near the school, I saw the bush where I had peed and suddenly I remembered something. I had left a video under the bush. Today I had remembered. Not the day Donny gave it to me, but today. One thing I didn't forget though was that Donny told me not to tell anyone about the video, but I wasn't going to anyway because no one would let me play the game. And I wanted to play it.

I found a pen in my father's glove compartment and wrote down a 'V' on my arm, so this time I wouldn't forget.

My dad glanced over at me and smiled. "Is that for *victory*?" he asked.

I nodded. Sure. Why not, I thought. My dad drove into the parking lot of the school and after he'd parked, I opened the car door. There wasn't another car in the parking lot.

"Thanks for the ride," I said.

"Hey, if it's okay, I thought I'd help you. Maybe run with you." He cut the engine and patted his stomach. "I could use the exercise. I used to have to run lines for football. I could jog with you and time you as you do sprints."

I shrugged. "Okay," I said.

We both got out and walked to the track. My dad wasn't someone who talked a lot, unlike my mother who talked all the time, so we just walked side by side.

"I'm proud of you," he said.

"How come?" I asked.

He put his arm around me. "You're doing a great job on this track team. Sam says you're working really hard."

"I like the races best."

"Yeah, it's like any sport. The race or the game is always the best thing and the part that keeps you practising. But you do have to practise. Of course, it has to be fun too. That counts for a lot."

My dad ran around the track with me a few times, maybe four, but he had to stop because he said it was a long time since he'd run. Then he said I should do some stops and starts, and he would maybe run again later. The stuff he had me do was kind of like the stuff I had done with Mr. Rossi where I ran and walked.

I lined up and got in my crouch and he yelled *GO*. I took off, going as fast as I could. Then he yelled *STOP* and I walked. It was different than doing it at track practice because I wasn't running beside anyone, so it made it harder to keep going. After I'd gone a couple of times around the track, my dad called out to me.

"One more time," he said.

"It's boring," I said.

He walked over to me. "Okay. I understand. You just needed to break in your shoes anyways. You did a good job." He smiled at me. "You're going to be great this week at the school meet. You want to run once more around, maybe as a cool-down? I think I could manage another lap if we went slow."

I looked down at my arm and saw the V that I had written. Video games weren't boring, especially the one Donny gave me. I had to get it.

"I'm going to run home," I said.

"That's a great idea," said my dad. "Good cool-down." He gave me a playful punch on the arm. "Plus, I didn't really want to run another lap anyway."

I laughed and gave him a little punch back. We always play like this. Back and forth, we jabbed each other, just for fun. He always says it has to be just for fun. Then he managed to get me in a headlock and he rubbed my head. Then we jabbed a bit more and I got him in a headlock and rubbed his head. He laughed.

"Let me go!" He laughed and laughed.

I was laughing too. I did let him go and he said, "I'll follow you home in the car."

I glanced around, trying to figure out how I was going to get the video game without him seeing.

"You can go," I said.

"I should follow you."

My dad and I walked to his car and he got in and I started to run. He honked his horn and I waved to him. When we got home we both went into the house. Then I told him I was going to have a shower. I pretended to go to my room but when he went in the kitchen I snuck out the back door. Then I ran like crazy back to the school.

When I was in front of the bush, I got down on my knees and felt around in the dirt under the biggest branch. I felt and I felt. My hand scratched along the dirt. I couldn't find it. I kept patting the dirt. Finally, I laid down and tried to look. I saw it! Pushed way at the back. I wiggled closer until my hand felt the plastic, then I pulled it out.

I couldn't wait to get home and play it.

Holding the video, I ran home but when I got close to my house I knew I had to figure out how to get it inside. I didn't have a PlayStation in my room, so I would have to go to Declan's room.

I went quietly in the back door and when I was sure no one had noticed me, I stuck it in my shorts and pulled my shirt overtop. Then I raced through the kitchen and scooted down the hall.

"I made you lemonade," my mother called out to me.

"Okay, hang on," I said. I went into the washroom and got a towel and wrapped the game in it. I creaked open the washroom door and peered down the hallway. It was empty. I went to my room and stashed the video under my mattress.

Then I went to the kitchen and picked up a glass of lemonade, swigging it down in three big gulps. I wiped my mouth with my hand.

"I thought Dad said you were having a shower," she said. Then she looked me up and down. "Why are your clothes so dirty?"

I looked down at my shirt and saw that it was stained brown from the dirt. "I dunno."

She narrowed her eyes at me. "It looks like you were crawling on the ground. Or did you fall?" She bent down to look at my knees. "No scratches."

"I fell but didn't hurt myself." I backed away from her. "Where's Dad?"

"He's still in the shower." She laughed. "You wore him out."

"Is Declan home?"

"No. Declan is working today. He started his job. Remember when he left this morning?" She smiled.

I thought about him leaving, wearing a blue shirt that said Best Buy. "I hope he brings home a video."

"Stuart, he can't just take things from the store now that he works there. Even as an employee, he will have to pay for things."

"That sounds like a shitty job."

"Hey, watch your language." She wagged her finger at me. Whenever I swore, she always told me to *watch my language.*

"Have you been listening to music you're not supposed to?" she asked.

"No," I said. "My teacher said it in class."

She frowned at me. "Is that the truth?"

I shrugged. "I dunno." I stood there for a second before I said, "Can I watch television? Dad said the golf was on."

"Sure," she said. "I have to go out and run an errand and pick up Declan, but Dad is staying home. If you need anything, ask him."

After she left, I went and had a shower. After my shower, I saw my dad and he was doing something in the garage.

I went to my room and got the video, then I tiptoed across the hall to Declan's room. He had a television in his room and he could only play video games on it. He was allowed a television because he didn't wreck things and my parents said he was *responsible* with his games. I wanted one too. But they thought I might break it and I wasn't allowed until I stopped punching my walls. Declan didn't punch walls. If he got mad he lifted weights in the garage.

I quietly closed the door and slipped the video into the PlayStation. I plunked down in front of it with the controller. When the screen lit up, my heart started racing and I stared at the zapping colours. The lights, the buzzing, the flash of red and yellow and black and deep purple made my body buzz too.

Focus. That's what Sam always said to me.

Fun. That's what my dad had said. If it was fun, it was okay. Playing this video game was fun! So that would make it okay.

I started playing at level 1 but wanted to get to level 2, which meant killing. Whoever got in my way. I used guns and knives and even hand knuckles to kill people. Make them bleed. Hold their wounds and die. *Die. Die.* I moved my body with the action and never let my eyes leave the screen.

Even when the door burst open.

I was on level 4 and was in mid-kill, so I didn't even look to see who it was. There was no way I could take my eyes off or else I would be killed.

"What are you doing in my room?" Declan grabbed the controller from my hand.

"Don't!" I tried to keep hold of the controller. I was almost on level 5! Then I got shot. Red blood spurted from my chest and I fell, clutching my heart where I'd been shot. A weird sound came from the television and it was like warped music. It meant I was slowly dying and soon would be completely dead.

"Why did you do that?" I screamed at Declan. "Now I'm dead. I would have made level 5!"

"Where'd you get this game?" He held up the case that the game had come in.

"None of your business." I scowled at him and tried to grab the case from his hand, but he put it behind his back.

"It's mine," I said.

"Where'd you get it? We don't even sell this game at Best Buy. It's too violent. It's rated the most violent game on all the lists."

"I like it," I yelled. "It's fun. Dad says things have to be fun."

"I'm telling him you're playing this game unless you tell me who gave it to you."

I exhaled through my teeth. He was making me *sooo* mad. I was ready to hit something or punch a hole in his wall. That's how mad I was. He just ruined me getting to level 5. I wanted to jump on him or punch him in the face. I made my hand into a fist and tried to slug him, but he grabbed my wrist and held on to it. He was so strong. I tried to kick him too, but he pushed me against the wall.

"Stop trying to hit me," he said. "I'm stronger than you. Now, who gave you that game?"

Declan stared me right in the eyes and I knew I was never going to be able to get away from him.

"Okay," I said. "Let me go and I'll tell you."

He dropped his arms and mine just fell to my side. Then I shook my arms, especially my wrist.

He was still standing in front of me, though, kind of like a wall. I thought I could try to duck under him, but he might grab me again.

"Okay," I said, through clenched teeth. "Donny did. But he told me not to tell."

"You're so stupid to see him." He shook his head at me and stepped back.

"I didn't see him. He just gave me that game."

"You're going to jail."

"I am not."

"Yeah, you are. If you keep hanging out with him. There was a kid in my class who hung out with a friend of Donny's and he's in *jail*. The kid robbed a grocery store and killed the store owner and went to jail for *murder*."

"Murder?"

"Donny told him to kill a real person instead of just a person on the video game. He has guns y'know. Have you seen his guns?"

"I dunno." I looked at the floor.

"You've seen his guns?"

"NO!"

"People get beat up in jail," he said. "Every day. You'll get beat up and you'll never see Mary's baby if you go to jail. You'll be a bad influence. You won't be an uncle."

"Shut up!"

Declan walked over to the PlayStation and pulled the game out of the machine, and before I could snatch it from his hands, he broke it in half. The snap was so loud and it made me so mad. I stomped out of his room, and went across the hall to my room. The first thing I saw was my walls, and I was about to punch one when my dad walked into my room.

"There you are," he said. "Mom told me to find you. She thought you were watching golf. But then she heard noise and thought you and Declan were fighting."

Air hissed out of me, and my arms felt like wet noodles, not arms that could punch a wall. They hung to my side.

"Are you watching golf?" I asked my dad without looking at him. Maybe he would watch it with me. In the summer we went golfing. I liked driving the cart the best.

"Yeah, I can," he said. "If you want to."

"Okay," I replied. "I want to."

On Monday, I went to school with my new running shoes because I had a track-and-field practice after school. After the last bell rang, Sam met me at the doors leading outside to the track-and-field area. I had made my way down to that door by myself because Tony had reminded me about my practice. And Mr. Rossi had seen me in the hall and stopped to talk to me. Teachers didn't usually stop to talk to me in the halls unless I was doing something wrong, like dodging people.

Outside, Mr. Rossi called us all over because he wanted to talk to us. Sam said that I was going to work with the other kids again today. I thought if that mean kid said anything to me, I was going to turn around and clock him one. I swear I would. Punch him hard.

I felt all angry inside, like my blood was moving too fast and my head was exploding. Declan had made me so mad, wrecking my game and telling me I was going to jail. He'd said that to me again this morning.

I stood at the back of the group when Mr. Rossi was talking. Sam tried to get me to go to the front, but I wouldn't budge forward. I didn't want to. I started to get all jittery with him telling me to move forward. Why didn't people listen to me when I said I didn't want to do something?

"No," I said. "I want to stand here."

"But you can't see."

"I don't care," I said loudly. All the kids turned to stare at me. "Stop staring," I said.

Sam leaned in to me. "It's okay," he said. "You can stay where you are."

I sort of listened but it was hard to do when so many things were bubbling. I felt like a firecracker was going to go off inside of me.

At the end of Mr. Rossi's talk, Sam leaned in and said, "Do you understand what you're going to be doing?"

"I dunno."

"It's similar to the other day, where you run fast, then run slow, then run fast again. And you're going to be working with the blocks today with the other runners.

"Okay," I said. I liked that.

I lined up where Mr. Rossi and Sam said to line up, and I was beside the boy who didn't like me. He pushed me a little and moved in front of me. Like, stood *right in front of me* so I couldn't see. Now I wanted to see and didn't want him standing in front of me. I didn't like that he did that.

The whistle blew and everyone started running. I tried to start like everyone else, but the boy pushed me again. After I'd righted my body, I ran. The whistle blew and I slowed down like I was supposed to. Then it blew again and I was ready.

I ran hard, like really hard, because I was going to go by that kid and nail him one. Push him like he pushed me. As I went by him, I was on the outside, so I used my elbow to shove him, and he was running so fast, he tripped and went flying on the grass beside the track.

The whistle blew and I kept running instead of stopping. I didn't care. I ran by a whole bunch of kids.

"Hey, kid, you're supposed to walk now!"

I heard the boy behind me yelling. "That stupid kid pushed me on purpose! He should be kicked off the team!"

Sam was on the inside of the track and I could see him coming toward me. He cupped his hands around his mouth. "Stuart, slow down. The whistle blew!"

So I did. I stopped running and just walked. Like everyone else. But then Mr. Rossi called us all in and the kid who fell got up and wiped grass off his legs. I heard Mr. Rossi asking him if he was okay and he said he was and then he said some mean things about me. I didn't care. He'd pushed me first.

Sam came over and walked beside me. "Why did you push him?" he whispered.

"Because he pushed me first," I said.

"That's what I thought," he said quietly. He didn't say anything else to me and now we had to go and listen to Mr. Rossi again. He talked about how we couldn't push each other on the track because we all belonged on the same team, even though we would be competing against each other. Made no sense.

"Why are we on the same team?" I asked Sam. "We always go against each other."

"Because you're from the same school. The school gets points at the city meet with the other schools," said Sam. "If the school gets the most points then everyone from our school wins."

Now we had to walk over to the start line because we were going to practise on the blocks. Finally, something fun to do.

Sam continued talking, "You do have to win something at our school event on Thursday, though, to be part of the team that goes to the city meet. You do remember you are racing Thursday, right? Your family is coming to watch."

I nodded. I did remember that because it was written on the calendar in our kitchen, and my mother made me read the calendar every day.

"That will be fun," I said. "As long as I'm not beside that stupid kid who pushed me."

Sam stopped me from walking and turned me to face him. He grabbed my shoulders and looked at me. "If you are beside him, ignore him and beat him. Just run by him. That's better than any push."

I nodded.

"You're going to love racing on Thursday. That's where you'll shine. And if before Thursday someone pushes you, you just tell me, instead of sending the guy flying off the track. That kid is worried you're going to take his spot. Stuff like that happens in sports. Believe me, I know."

I nodded. "If he does it again and I tell you, what will you do to him?"

"I won't push him back, but I'll talk to Mr. Rossi, okay?"

I shrugged. I was going to work with the blocks now, so I didn't really care.

The blocks were all set up and Mr. Rossi told eight of us to go to them, while the others did exercises on the grass—those high legs and mountain climbers and stuff I didn't want to do. I was glad to be going out of the blocks. I put my one leg back and my other leg forward, just like Sam had shown me. I put my fingers on the ground and looked straight ahead.

Mr. Rossi said, "On your marks. Set. *GO.*"

I flew out of the blocks and ran five steps. Just like he told me to do.

The next time, Mr. Rossi said that instead of saying *GO* he was going to use a GUN. We were going to practise with a GUN. Because that's how the race would be started on Thursday. I wanted to see the gun. Touch it. Shoot it. Yes, I wanted to shoot the gun.

While everyone set up, Sam came up behind me. "Do you understand about the gun?" he asked me, and I barely heard him because he spoke so quietly.

I nodded. "Can I see the gun?" I wondered if it was like Donny's.

Uh oh. Donny. If I saw him again I was going to jail.

"Not right now. I'll make sure you can see it afterwards. Are you okay with that?"

"Can't I see it now?" *What if it was one of Donny's guns?*

"Not now. Later, okay? Do the practice with it and I will ask if you can see the gun after."

Mr. Rossi told us to get in our blocks. So I did. And I crouched. And stared straight ahead.

Donny had a gun. Donny made kids go to jail.

Suddenly, I heard a noise, a car noise. A loud car with two exhaust pipes, that went fast.

I glanced around. *Where was Donny? Was he on the road? Was he behind the dumpster? What if he made me go to jail!*

What if he had his gun with him?

"On your marks!" Mr. Rossi yelled.

I looked over at Mr. Rossi and saw the gun pointed in the air.

Was that Donny's gun? I couldn't tell! Was he going to shoot Donny?

"Set!" Mr. Rossi yelled.

I heard the car and the gun go off at the same time. I exploded out of the blocks and ran. And ran and ran and ran.

I didn't want to go to jail. Declan told me I would.

145

Donny couldn't see me. If I saw him, I could go to jail.

Because I'd seen his GUN.

I kept running. And didn't stop at the finish line. I hopped over the side of the track and ran toward the front of the school. I needed a place to hide. Under the bushes.

CHAPTER FOURTEEN
SAM

Where was he going?

"Stuart!" I called, but he just kept running.

Oh, man. Had the gun spooked him? I had totally forgotten about how Mr. Rossi practised with the gun a couple of days before the meet. He'd done the same thing every year. Who knows what Stuart had been through when he was little? Maybe someone had shot a gun in one of the other houses he lived in before being adopted by the Williams family. The kid had been fostered in some good homes but also in some really bad homes too. Plus, his home with his real mother must have been awful. His mother had tried to drown him. Who does that?

I had to do something.

"I'll go get him," I said to Mr. Rossi.

I started off jogging when really I wanted to run full tilt. I hated this heart thing. I couldn't do anything. Like, *anything*. I gritted my teeth and clenched my fists to stop myself from running all out. My insides felt choked and my head throbbed.

I could still see Stuart up ahead, so I called to him again. He did look over his shoulder as if he'd heard me, so I waved at him. He stopped and looked around. I kept jogging, but I also glanced around. What was he looking for? He cranked his head and seemed to be scanning the streets, up and down. Then he dove under a bush.

"Stuart! Stay there!"

I continued my slow jog over to him. Every time I increased my speed, I started panting so I slowed down. Fortunately, he wasn't moving from under the bush.

Stay there. Stay there. Please, stay where you are. I kept muttering to myself as I walked. Finally, I reached the bush and squatted down, flipping up a branch. He was sitting with his arms around his legs, rocking back and forth.

"Hey," I said, trying to act normal and subdued instead of panicked. "Come on out."

He looked at me, then he crawled out from under the bush.

"What happened, dude? Did the gun scare you?"

"I dunno."

When he gave me his blank, "I dunno," I knew better than to ask more questions. "Maybe we should call it a day and just go out front of the school and wait for your ride."

"But I want to go back and work with the blocks," he said.

"Okay. Let's go talk to Mr. Rossi."

We slowly walked back and didn't talk because I didn't want to bug him. I wanted to give him time to tell me what had happened. If it was the gun, perhaps I could practise with him, although, where would I get a gun? Maybe I could put a gun sound on my phone?

We walked at a snail's pace and Stuart kept stopping and looking around or stopping to tie up his shoe or pull up his sock.

Muddled in thoughts that were running zig-zags through my head, I approached Mr. Rossi as he was ending the practice. I saw Cecil across the field and he gave me a wave and a funny gesture as if to say, "What happened?"

I waved back to him and pointed to Mr. Rossi, letting him know we were going to talk to him.

"Stuart," said Mr. Rossi. "What happened?"

"I dunno."

"Was it the gun?"

He nodded.

"Okay. It's a good thing we practised. Is your mom picking you up?"

Stuart looked up at Mr. Rossi. "Can I practise with the blocks now?"

"Sure. I'd like to talk to Sam for a few minutes, so you go over and do a few starts."

When Stuart was out of earshot, Mr. Rossi looked at me and said, "I'm not sure this is going to work."

"But he's been working hard," I said. "And he's *fast*. I can keep working with him. I promise he can do it. I think he just got spooked by the gun. Who knows what happened to him early in his life? If I go over and over it with him, I think he'll be okay."

"You can't promise that." He put a hand on my shoulder, which was so not him.

"I really think he can do it." I said. "I believe in him."

"Look, Sam, he pushed Claude off the track. What if he does that when he's in a race with someone from another school?"

"That's not fair," I said. "Claude pushed him first. You didn't see that part. Stuart isn't sneaky—he doesn't know how to do stuff like that without getting caught. Claude does."

"He must have provoked him," said Mr. Rossi.

Provoked? Seriously Mr. Rossi, dude. You're going to use the word provoked.

"Look, Mr. Rossi. I know Stuart is hyper and unpredictable, but whatever. The thing is, he doesn't provoke stuff; he reacts."

Mr. Rossi was still looking pretty skeptical. He needed to see the whole picture here.

"Claude thinks he's going to lose his chance to compete in the city meet because of Stuart," I said. "So, he shoved him first. Kids bully Stuart all the time because of who he is."

Mr. Rossi tucked his clipboard under his arm. "I'll think about it tonight. Come see me tomorrow." And that was that. He walked away from me.

I ran my hand through my hair as I stared at Stuart, who was blasting out of the blocks and talking to himself. Finally, I walked over to him.

"Good job," I said to him. "Remember to use your legs. Dig in and push."

"Is Mr. Rossi mad at me?" He hung his head.

I hated seeing him do that. "No," I said.

He looked up at me, his eyes full of this weird sadness that seriously made me feel his pain. And that's not a lie. Something hit me in the gut, like I'd been sucker punched too. The kid needed a chance. So, he'd been spooked by a gun. I'd practise with him somehow, some way.

"Can I run on Thursday?" he asked.

I smiled at him. "Of course you can run, Little Man," I said. Then I held up my hand. "And you're going to kick some butt!"

He slapped my hand back.

Man, I hoped I could deliver on that promise.

After dinner, I went to my room and started pacing back and forth, like a caged animal. Back and forth, wearing down the carpet.

I picked up my phone and reread all the texts Bethany had sent. We'd had such a good time, or I had for sure, on Friday night. We'd texted on Saturday, back and forth, just talking about stuff, like what we had planned for the day.

Then on Sunday, after she'd told me about her flag football game that she'd played in the park, everything came crashing down in my mind. Some boyfriend I'd be for an athletic girl like her. I couldn't compete with the jocks of the world.

I hadn't answered one of her texts since then. Not one. I'd read them and not answered. What a dick. I'd watched television all day Sunday and ignored her.

Now, I desperately wanted to talk to her. Had I blown it?

I tossed my phone back and forth and back and forth. My stomach felt sick, like I wanted to barf. She was the one I wanted to talk to first about all of this because I knew she would understand.

I composed a text then deleted it. Composed another one. Deleted it too. Another and another.

Finally, I made it simple.

hey how was football?

I waited, staring at my phone, pacing, pacing. Would she text me back?

The phone pinged. I glanced down.

good

That was it? All she was going to say? My heart sank to my toes. I tried to breathe to calm myself down. I could do this. My throat dried but I made my fingers go to work.

Wanna chat???

Was I being too bold? Being too needy? Being too…

sure give me a call now

Before I lost my nerve, I called her.

"Hey," I said. My voice seriously cracked like I was fourteen all over again. "How you doing?"

"Great," she said. Her voice sounded okay. Not mad. Or was I just hoping for the best? Maybe I was making too big a deal out of me not texting. Maybe she wasn't that type of girl who got mad when you didn't respond. So many maybes were banging in my head like a bad drum roll that I must have forgotten to speak.

"What's up?" she asked.

"I'm sorry I didn't text back."

"Why didn't you? It's not hard to answer a text."

"Um, you were playing flag football." What a lame thing to say. "It's something I can't really do anymore."

"Who cares? It's just flag football."

"I know." I exhaled. "I guess I care. I used to be able to do all that stuff."

"You can talk to me about this anytime, you know." Her usually low, gravelly voice sounded soft.

"Sure," I said quickly. "I really wanted to talk to you about Stuart today though." I flopped back on my bed and told her the story of Stuart and how the sound of the gun had made him take off. The words just flowed out of me.

The one thing I left out, though, was the fact that I'd *promised* him he could run.

"They have to let him run," I said. "They just have to. He'll be so disappointed if he can't."

There was silence on the other end. Then she said, "Why don't you bring him out to Special Olympics? It might be easier for him. It's a gradual ease-in and everyone involved wants the best from the athletes, so we work with them, both mentally and physically."

"I know he can do this," I said, thumping the bed with my fist. "He can run in this track meet Thursday and he can beat some of these kids. He can."

More silence. Then she said, "But does he want to? Does he really want to? Or is he doing this to make you happy?"

"I think he does." I stood up and started my pacing again. "In fact, I know he does."

"Okay," she said. "Then stick with him. Maybe take the pressure off. Make it more fun."

"But I will bring him to Special Olympics," I said. "I mean he might do really well there too. And the school meets will end in a few weeks. We have our school meet Thursday and Cities are the following Thursday. A bus takes all the athletes over and it would be a huge deal for him." I was rambling a little, but I couldn't stop myself. "But I could bring him Friday night maybe, after the school meet. Just for fun."

"Sure," she said. "That sounds good. Just play it by ear. Best way to operate."

The following Friday seemed like a long way away. Just talking to her made me want to see her again. I didn't really want to wait. Should I ask her to go for coffee, again? Or ice cream? Or for a walk even? Just a walk. I wasn't doing anything all night. *Nada.* Lying on my bed. Sunset was getting later every night. She really was only one bus away.

"Um," I started. "Um," I said again. "You wanna go for a walk?" I got the words out. I held my breath.

"Tonight? You're kidding right?"

"Um." My heart did a huge belly flop and it stung.

"It's not that I don't want to," she said, "but it's the seventh game of the Raptors-Miami series! Aren't you watching? This game is huge for them."

Yeah, I knew about it but had been trying to forget. Cecil had asked me to go to his house but I'd said no. "Um, yeah, huge game."

"I am so excited! Like. So. Excited! But I've been so swamped with stuff that I didn't make plans to have friends over like I usually do," she said. "Plus it's a Monday and I'm always on babysitting duty, so a full-blown party at my place is a little out unless it's miniscule. My mom takes an accounting class on Monday night, so I have to be home for my little brother and sister. But…" she paused but just for a split-second, "you know, if *you* wanted to come to my place and watch I think that'd be cool. One person isn't exactly a party but we're ordering pizza."

"Oh, okay," I said. I got off my bed and paced in my room. "Okay." I really did want to see her. But to watch a game? Dilemma.

I sucked in a deep breath before I said, "What's your address?"

After she'd given it to me, she said, "Wear your jersey!" And if you don't have one, I have an extra. Just don't come in Miami gear. You won't get in my house."

"You bet. See ya." I pressed end on my phone and exhaled. Not a big deal. Of course I had a jersey, so I pulled it from the back part of my closet and put it on. Then I went downstairs. Did I dare ask my dad for a ride? He had the television on and looked up when he saw me come into the television room.

"Ahh, you finally watch game," he said, giving me a thumbs-up. He always looked so awkward when he tried to do "cool" things and I laughed.

"I'm going out," I said.

"You go to some friend house?"

"Uh, yeah," I said.

"I give you ride."

"Um, sure," I said. A ride would be nice but the explanation of where I was going, not so nice.

He got out of his chair and looked at his watch. "We go. I don't want to miss nothing."

In the car, I used the GPS on my phone and discovered Bethany didn't live too far away. Fifteen minutes max. I guided my father, and he didn't ask a lot of questions as we drove and the few he did, I gave vague answers to. When we got to the house, I quickly got out of the car.

"Thanks, Dad," I said.

"You need ride home?"

I shrugged. "I can take the bus."

"Call. I pick you up."

I nodded and slammed the door. Then I walked up the sidewalk and took the three steps to the front door. I turned around before I knocked and saw my father was just pulling away. Good.

Bethany answered the door wearing a Raptors jersey that hung to her knees, and behind her stood a boy who looked around eight or so, with a huge grin on his face and a Raptors hat on backwards.

"Who are you?" the boy asked.

"Logan, that's rude," said Bethany. She shook her head and tousled his hair, a good tousle too. Then she looked at me. "I'll apologize now for his behaviour."

He screwed up his face, moved out of her reach, then body-checked her. "Don't say that!"

She howled with laughter.

"Hi, Logan," I said, smiling at him.

"That's enough, Logan. Fun's over," said Bethany, moving aside. "Come on in. I told my mom you were coming and she said it was okay."

"Yeah, cuz Bethany's not allowed *boys* over when she babysits us but she said you were a friend from Best Buddies so my mom said yes."

"Too much information, dude," she said to Logan. "Now go. Remember what I said. You bug me, you don't get pepperoni pizza. I'll order all veggie."

He crossed his arms across his chest and frowned, but then he did run away.

"Works every time," she said.

I took off my shoes in the front entrance. Then she led the way to a room that was off the kitchen and definitely the family room. Family photos hung on the wall, including school and sports photos. I studied one of Bethany in her soccer outfit with a big "C" on the shirt. She was holding an MVP trophy.

"Glad you wore a jersey," she said.

"Thanks." I pointed to the photo. "You said you played soccer, but I didn't know you were a star."

"Whatever," she said. "Team sports. Everyone is a star."

I nodded. "Yeah, that's how I always felt."

"You can feel that way again, you know." She tilted her head and stared directly into my eyes.

"I can't—"

She made the slashing movement to her throat, stopping me mid-sentence. "Don't say what I think you're going to say. You may not get that high from being an athlete when you coach, but you sure get something that resembles it." She pointed to a big comfy chair that had these red Raptors shaker things and red Styrofoam hands. "You can take anything you want. The game is about to start." Then she put her fingers to her mouth and whistled.

Logan came running into the room and he was now dressed in some sort of Raptor costume, looking a little like the mascot.

I burst out laughing. "You guys are real fans."

"Oh, yeah," said Bethany, lifting her hand up to high-five Logan. "Logan and I love watching sports on television."

He jumped and smacked her hand so hard I thought she'd topple over, but she didn't. She stood solid.

Since the photos on the wall showed three kids, I said, "What about your sister?"

Logan howled like a hyena. "She doesn't like sports. Not one bit," he said. "Like not even a little bit. Not even an inch of a bit. All she likes is boring old studying."

Bethany shrugged. "What can I say? We're all different. She's up in her room with her headphones on. We're all good to go here. I'll take her up some pizza when it arrives."

The game started and I found myself on the sofa with Logan *in between* me and Bethany. Logan bounced around like a small puppy looking for treats, on his knees, off his knees, up and down. And Bethany sat forward and didn't take her eyes off the television.

I watched the game like I used to watch games, with a critical eye, but I also watched Bethany. She seriously jumped up and cheered every time the Raptors stole the ball, and when they got a basket she waved her foam hand like a maniac. And she talked to the television, telling the players to get moving or get in position, and she told the refs off.

"That wasn't a foul!" she yelled halfway through the first quarter. The Raptors' best player was on his second foul and they were down by five.

"Agreed," I said. She was right. It was a dubious call.

"No way. How could he make that call? The guy went up with him but didn't touch him." She turned to me. "What a pile of poop."

I burst out laughing. "I can't believe you just said that."

"She's not allowed to swear around me," said Logan.

I laughed so hard, I almost spit water out of my mouth.

She reached over Logan and batted me with her foam hand. I pretended to be hurt. "Ouch," I said.

"That wouldn't hurt," said Logan.

"Did you play basketball?" I asked Bethany. "You know a lot."

She snorted. "Me? Have you checked my height? I'm 5'2. I tried in junior high but the coach cut me, even though I thought I was better than the girl who was 5'7. They picked the team based on height only. So I decided to stick with soccer."

"Probably smart."

Since a commercial was on she looked over at me. "What about you? Any other sports?"

"I tried just about everything but hockey. My parents didn't have the money for equipment."

"I play hockey," said Logan.

"I can see that." I pointed to his hockey photos on the wall.

"I play basketball with Dillon sometimes," said Bethany. "Just simple games of 21."

"Yeah, I used to play with Stuart."

"Didn't you say you could still play recreationally?"

"Yeah." I picked at a thread on my shirt.

"Let's get Dillon and Stuart together for a little game of basketball. It would be fun. You don't have to run after the ball because they will."

Fortunately, I didn't have to answer because the doorbell rang and both Bethany and Logan jumped up to go get the pizza.

I ran into Cecil the next morning at school, and before I could think, I said, "What a game last night!"

"You watched it, dude?" He playfully punched my shoulder. "And you didn't call me!"

"Yeah, I saw it."

"Did your dad stronghold you and make you watch?"

"Something like that," I said.

"I'm glad to hear you're back to the land of the living, bro. Okay, so how about that three-point shot at the end? Holy mackerel, was it a shot to behold!" Cecil used his hands to talk then he jumped in the air and pretended to take a shot himself.

And just like that we were talking about the game, the NBA, and all the teams left in the playoffs. It felt okay. Well, more than okay. Like something had returned. I still wasn't sure about playing though, and I hadn't given Bethany an answer about a game of 21. Not sure I wanted to pick up a basketball ever again in my life—to hold it, feel it. I didn't want the longing to return.

After my first class, I met up with Mr. Rossi to talk to him about Stuart, like he'd asked me to the day before. I knocked on his door.

"Come on in."

"Hi, Mr. Rossi," I said.

"Sam, good to see you. Have a seat."

Uh oh. Having to take a seat meant we needed to have a chat.

"I'm not sure this is going to work with Stuart," he said. "Maybe the school meet just isn't the right event for him. He seems to do well at the Best Buddies events. Maybe keep him there."

"I think he can do it," I said.

Mr. Rossi leaned back in his chair and swirled his pencil around his finger. "I know you do. But we have to be realistic."

"Please, let me keep trying. It's just the school meet. If it doesn't go well, then he won't make Cities, and that's the end of it."

He sighed noisily and leaned forward. "Okay. We'll give this one more go. He deserves it. He's worked hard."

"Thank you so much." I stood up.

I had my hand on the doorknob when he said, "You should probably go over the gun with him again. And also false starts."

"Right," I said.

"You can handle that? Because I can help if you need me to."

"I can do it," I said. "But thanks."

At lunch my mission was to find Stuart. When I didn't see him in the cafeteria, I went to the room where his aide often ate lunch with him. There he was, doing some sort of work.

"Can I talk to him?" I asked Tony.

"He's supposed to be doing his work."

"No, I'm not," said Stuart.

"Well, you are but…" Tony looked at me. "Have at it," he said with a shrug. "He's in a bit of a mood today. Right, Stuart?"

"Yeah," he said. "I'm in a bad mood all right."

Tony shook his head and said, "I'll go get a coffee. I know you got new shoes with turbo jets but no running, okay?" He gave Stuart a wink and a smile, obviously trying to get him to smile back.

Since Tony worked with Stuart every day, I thought I would ask him the best way to teach Stuart about false starts. "Can I talk to you for a second?"

"Sure. Stuart," he said. "Do one more question, okay?"

"I. DON'T. WANT. TO!"

When we were out of Stuart's earshot, I said, "I have to teach him about false starts before the track-and-field meet. Any suggestions? I don't want to stress him out, but he needs to understand what they mean."

Tony shook his head. "I wouldn't right now. He's in a mood and he might fixate on it and not run at all. Wait until he's a little calmer."

I nodded. "Thanks," I said.

I went back to Stuart and sat down across from him. His arms were tightly wrapped around his chest and he had a huge scowl on his face.

"What's up, Little Man?" I asked.

"Mary is going to have her baby and I'm not going to be able to be an uncle."

"Why not?"

"Declan said so. He told me I was going to jail."

Okay, so this was something new, I thought. I'd never heard him talk about jail before. How to deal with this? Was he telling the truth or was this something he saw on television?

Questions. I was always supposed to ask him questions if he was in a mood. And give him choices so he made decisions. His parents had talked to me on the phone before we joined Best Buddies. Anger issues were part of his FASD, among other things, like running away when things didn't add up for him.

"Why did he say that?" I asked.

He shrugged and looked down at the table. I waited for the "I dunno" but he just slouched and slid lower in his chair.

"I'm sure he didn't mean it," I said.

He scratched his thighs, his jeans, for a few seconds and I waited for him to say something. The noise of fingers against denim echoed in the small room. Over and over. Up and down. I just sat there and watched him and listened to him scratching, wondering what he scratched in the summer when he wore shorts. The table? Walls?

Finally, he stopped, looked up, and said, "Do I get to run?"

"You do," I said. "I just talked to Mr. Rossi and he said a-okay." I held up my thumb. "Do you still want to?" I will admit, after seeing him like this, a part of me wondered if it might be better if he just said no.

When he didn't answer right away, I said, "I'll be there to help you. I believe in you, Little Man."

He nodded. "I want to," he said. His scowl had disappeared, and the corners of his mouth actually lifted a little to give me the smallest of smiles.

I held up my hand. "It's a deal. You're on, dude."

He slapped it so hard, I almost fell off my chair, or at least I pretended to. Stuart was so interesting because his mood could change in seconds.

Since Tony hadn't returned, I pulled out the cards. "Snap or…" I leaned closer, "Blackjack?"

Now, he grinned. "Blackjack!"

We played a couple of hands before I said anything about the track-and-field meet.

"Listen," I said, as I shuffled the cards. "On Thursday, you can't run away, okay?"

"Okay," he mumbled.

"I'm serious. And you can't just run off the track in the middle of the race either. If you want to win the race you have to go to the finish line. You did it on your first day of practice so I know you can do it again. There's a time to run and a time not to run."

He looked at me with his head tilted sideways as if he really was listening, and perhaps he understood. I knew he often only hears snippits of sentences and not the entire thing.

"You understand that, right? So, in the race, you can run to the finish line. Always. At school, you can't run in the halls."

A grin, which resembled a mischievous smirk, appeared on his face. "I know that," he said. "But it's fun. I dodge people."

"But you know to go straight, right? When you're racing?"

He furrowed his eyebrows. "Not always. When I run the 400 I have to go around corners."

I burst out laughing and instantly felt relieved. "You're right. Just stay in your lane for every event that you are running. Between the white lines. And you will start with a gun, just like you did at practice last night. Remember: Only go with the gun shot."

"I know, I know!"

Okay, perhaps I had gotten the point across and Tony was right. I didn't need to discuss false starts just yet. "And don't push anyone, okay? Don't even touch anyone who is beside you."

"That kid doesn't like me."

"That's okay. Not everyone has to like you."

"That's what my mom says too." He paused before he said, "Let's play another hand. I want to beat you."

We played until Tony returned, which was close to bell-time. I gathered my things and made my way to math class. As I was walking down the hall, I decided to text Bethany and tell her that I'd convinced Mr. Rossi to let Stuart run. As I was using my thumbs and walking, head down, I felt a bump on my shoulder.

"Your mama again?" Cecil laughed.

I quickly pressed send before I shoved my phone in my back pocket. "Nah. Just someone with that Special Olympics program."

"Uh-huh. Yeah, right, bro. You don't fool me." He fingers to make quotation marks: *"That Special Olympics program."* Cecil laughed and slapped my back. "Who is she? Come clean, my man."

"Okay," I said. "I met her through a Best Buddies event. She doesn't go to our school."

"You seeing her?"

"Nah, nothing serious. I watched the game with her last night but her little brother was there too."

"You watched the game with a *chick*?" He shook his head. "That's gotta be a first. And she wasn't complaining or talking about stuff that had nothing to do with b-ball?"

"She knew more stats than you and me combined."

"Go on. You're pulling me."

"I'm not, Cec."

"Gift from the gods. When do I get to meet her?"

"How about never." I laughed and hip-checked him, sending him flying across the hallway.

CHAPTER FIFTEEN
STUART

The day before the track meet, I sat in my math class. It wasn't just Tony and me but other kids too. But Tony always had to join me.

He pointed to my math question. "We did this one yesterday," he said. "You got it right."

There were a bunch of kids in my math class who were also in the Best Buddies club at school. Tony had to work with more than just me. He worked with Gloria too and she didn't know how to do math either. Neither did Madeline, although she was probably better than me and Gloria. I liked Gloria because she told funny jokes, sometimes dirty ones (my mom got mad at me at home if I told them) that made most of us laugh. Tony worked with some of us, but we had a teacher too, Miss Ellis, who tried to get us to do math. She was the one who gave us the problems and then we were supposed to work on them, and Tony would go around and help, and so would the teacher.

I stared at the numbers. They didn't make any sense. I looked and looked at them. They just seemed to sit on the page like lumps. I had no idea what to do with them. Not a clue. I pushed my book away from me.

"Remember how you figured this out yesterday? You added this number with this." Tony pointed to one number on the page and then to another number. "You can do it again today."

I kept staring. If I tried, I could get it. Maybe. Then I looked at the clock. "I'm hungry."

"Five minutes until lunch bell," said Tony.

"I'm getting french fries today," said Gloria.

"Yooou get Freeench Friiies eveeery daaay," said Madeline.

"Do you guys have a Best Buddies dodgeball game today?" Tony asked.

"Dodgeball!" I jumped out of my chair. I didn't want to do math anymore. I wanted to go to the gym and play dodgeball. And eat my lunch.

"Sit down for just a few more minutes," said Miss Ellis. She came over to me and made me go back to my seat.

"Tony is right," she said. "You got the answer to this problem yesterday."

I chewed on the end of my pencil as I looked down at the numbers. Miss Ellis showed me what to do again and I stared and stared. Finally, something happened.

"I got it!" I yelled. "I got it!" I started to write down the answer.

"Good for you," said Miss Ellis.

The bell rang and I closed my book. "I'm done," I said.

I was shoving my book in my backpack when Sam came into the room. "Hey, dude. You ready for dodgeball? I just talked to Justin and he said he's got a surprise for everyone."

"I'm ready," I said, slinging my backpack on my shoulder.

"Okay, we'll eat first then we'll go."

I gobbled down my lunch and then Sam and I went down to the gym. When we got there, a lot of the Best Buddy kids were already there. Some must have eaten their lunches in the gym. Justin was making sure that everyone put their trash in the trash can.

Anna, who is Best Buddies with Harrison and is like a math wizard, came up to us. "We're so glad you guys are back," she said. "We missed you."

It seemed like a long time since I'd been at dodgeball. "I haven't been here since Christmas," I said.

"We were here after Christmas," said Sam, patting me on the back. "We've only not been here since..." he paused and I looked at him. He put his hand on his chest. "Since I got this hunk of metal put in me."

Then he crossed his arms and turned to Anna. "So, what's the surprise?"

"Yeah, what's the surprise?" I asked.

She smiled at me. "Just you wait."

Soon the gym was filled with kids and we were all playing soccer for fun before we played dodgeball, and we were running and kicking the ball.

I was the fastest runner and beat everyone to the ball. Gloria laughed every time she kicked it and missed. Once she kicked it so hard she went flying and fell on her butt. She still laughed. Willa asked if she was okay. When Gloria still laughed, Willa told her she was as tough as they come, and helped her up. I just kept running because that's what I do best.

Then Justin called us all in to gather in a circle. He always did that. When everyone was in a big circle, he said, "One of our Best Buddies is running in the track-and-field meet on Thursday."

"That's me!" I stuck my arms in the air.

Erika put her arms in the air too and said, "Go, Stuart, Go!"

Then Anna went running over to where all the balls were in a trolley, the ones we used to play dodgeball. From behind the trolley, she pulled out a bunch of signs and brought them over to the group.

"We have made signs for everyone to take to the track-and-field meet, and we can hold them up when Stuart is running."

She held one up. It said, "Go, Stuart!" Another one said, "Go, Stuart, Go!"

I liked them!

Then she held up a couple more, like one that said, "Run Fast, Stuart!"

"I like that one best," I said.

"We made them in art class," said Erika.

"I was not a part of this project," said Harrison. "I'm not particularly fond of art class as it is too abstract."

"Erika and Madeline made them for everyone to use," said Gianni. "We can all still cheer, even the ones who didn't make the signs."

"I'll make sure to get the times that Stuart is running to everyone," said Sam. "He's in the 100, 200, and 400 metre races."

"Way to go, Stuart," said Gianni. "Three events! Wow."

"I was in three dance numbers," said Erika, holding up three fingers. "When Gianni and I were in *Grease*."

"Rock on, dude," said Willa.

"Now, time for some dodgeball," said Justin. "I'll be It first. Who wants to be It with me?"

Not me, I thought. I wanted to run away from the ball and try not to get caught. I win this game all the time.

On Thursday morning, my mother asked me so many questions at breakfast and I just wanted her to stop talking. She'd made me an egg because she said I needed protein. Then she made me a smoothie which had little pieces of green in it. I didn't drink it. I wanted toast, like I always had, with peanut butter.

"Do you have your new sneakers in your backpack?" she asked. "And your shorts and t-shirt?"

"I dunno."

"Can I check your backpack? I washed your t-shirt last night and told you to put it in your bag."

I kept taking bites of my toast and eating my egg. Everyone was acting weird around me because I was running today. I didn't care if she checked my backpack.

"Have at it," I said.

"Does that mean *yes*?"

"Holy shit, Mom. Why are you asking so many questions?"

She pointed her finger at me. "Language."

I bowed my head and continued eating.

When she came back to the kitchen, she had my backpack in her hand and the case for the video game that Donny had given me.

She frowned at me. "Where did this come from?"

"I dunno."

Just then Declan walked into the kitchen, his hair sticking up all over the place and wearing only his pajama bottoms.

My mom opened the box and there was nothing inside. "Where's the game?" she asked.

"I broke it," said Declan.

My mother turned back to me. "Who gave you this video game? Where did you get it?" She didn't talk loud or yell, so she wasn't mad.

"I dunno," I said.

"You do so," said Declan. "That stupid Donny guy did. He's in jail now, y'know."

"What?" *Jail*? Donny was in jail?

"He's in jail. Got caught and put in handcuffs."

"When did he go to jail?" I hadn't seen him in a long time. Since Christmas maybe. No, not that long. Since he'd given me the video game.

My mother sat down across from me. "It was on the news last night," she said. "Donatello Dunn was arrested for selling drugs."

"It was a huge drug bust," said Declan. "You're lucky you weren't with him. Or else you would have been thrown in a jail cell too. They showed it on television. Everyone in his house had to come out with a cop and they were in handcuffs. The cops surrounded his house and they had their guns drawn. Just like in a TV show."

"Declan, I think that's enough," said my mom. "We can talk about this later."

"Handcuffs?" My brain was spinning. "Guns? At his house?"

Declan got out his Special K cereal and my mom poured him the rest of the smoothie she'd tried to pawn off on me.

"Stuart," said my mom as she handed Declan his smoothie. "That game he gave you is not a game you want to play."

I refused to look at her. Everyone was bugging me today. Asking so many questions about everything. And telling me all kinds of things that I didn't like.

I got up. "Stop talking to me!"

My mother sighed. "Okay. Sorry I brought this up. We'll talk later." She got up from the table. "On another note, good for you for putting your shoes and your shorts and t-shirt in your bag last night."

"I'm going to watch you today," said Declan, slurping his cereal. He always ate cereal for breakfast and he always made noises.

"So are lots of people," I said.

Not Donny though.

Not today because he was in jail.

The track-and-field meet didn't start until after announcements and the national anthem, "O Canada." Today, some kids sang on the microphone and they tried to make it like a hip-hop song but they weren't that good. Not as good as the rap music Donny played in his car.

When the anthem was finally over, Sam came and got me, and we walked to the changeroom so I could put on my shorts and t-shirt and shoes. My new shoes.

"Remember, you're starting with a gun," he said. "It's just like the word *GO*, only it's a gun shot. And don't go before it goes off, okay? That's a rule."

I shrugged. *Donny had guns. I'd seen them and held them. The cops had guns too.*

"Let's go outside and get you warmed up. You have heats in the morning and finals in the afternoon."

"Okay," I said.

"How are you feeling?" He put his arm around me.

I shrugged again. "Good."

"It's okay to be nervous. I'm always nervous before I play basketball—well, when I used to play basketball. So if your stomach is a little upset or you're feeling kind of jittery, that's okay. Just use all of that energy to run as fast as you can. In a straight line. Okay?"

"Except in the 200 and 400. In those races I go around corners."

"Right," he said, smiling at me.

I followed Sam outside and I couldn't believe how many people were at the track-and-field meet. There were even little stands selling water and other drinks. Kids were everywhere. Some events were already running, like high jump and shot put. I wasn't doing any of those events.

I saw a lot of parents and I looked for mine. Where were they? I looked and looked, but I couldn't see them. I had to squint to look for them because it was so sunny outside. I was glad I had a t-shirt under my jacket in case I got too hot.

"Here come your parents," said Sam.

"Where?" I said.

He pointed and I saw them and waved. They were all here. Randy was dressed in a suit, but he had his jacket slung over his shoulder. Mary waddled like she had something shoved up her butt. Owen was beside her, holding onto her arm. My mom and dad were both walking together, and my dad had his suit on too. When they saw me they waved and came over. Everyone was there but Declan, but he was probably still in the school. Lucky Declan got to graduate at the end of the year and not go to school anymore.

"How are you feeling?" my mom asked me.

"Why does everyone keep asking me that?" This was so confusing. I wasn't sick.

She smiled at me and pushed hair out of my eyes.

"I'm going to warm him up," said Sam to my family. He glanced at his watch. "He runs in his first heat in twenty minutes."

"We'll be at the finish line," said my dad. He gave me a thumbs-up and I gave him one back.

Sam and I walked away from my family and headed to an area that he said was quiet.

He made me stretch and do that mountain-climber exercise and high knees. Then I got to swing my leg back and forth and then the other leg, and I had to do that a couple of times. The stretches we did were stretches that Declan liked to do too.

Then he looked at his watch and said, "We'd better head over to the track."

We walked over to a great big, huge board that had all the lanes. Sam pointed to the board and there was my name. I was in lane six.

My stomach heaved up and down like it was doing cartwheels, one after the other. And I needed water; my throat was so dry. Was this what being nervous was all about? Sam had talked about being nervous. I also had the jitters. My body felt like it was vibrating.

Lane six. I was in lane six. I knew lane six.

"That's your lucky lane," said Sam.

I nodded.

"I can't go over there with you, Little Man. But you know what to do."

"Start running when the gun goes off and run in a straight line to the finish," I said.

He patted my back. "You got it!"

Mr. Rossi used a megaphone and called out, "Junior 100 metre boys. First heat. Line up at the start."

"That's you," said Sam. He patted my back and walked over toward where my family was.

I went over to lane six. I was okay with the boys beside me. Neither of them were mean to me. I put one foot against the back block and one foot on the front. I was supposed to take off low and just fly out of the blocks like a fast car.

Thinking of a fast car made me think of Donny. He was in jail. That's what Declan said. But I wasn't in jail. Declan said I would be if I hung out with him. Declan said I was going to jail.

"Runners, on your marks," yelled Mr. Rossi in the megaphone.

I wondered if Donny had killed someone with his gun. I saw his guns. I touched his guns.

"Set!" I heard Mr. Rossi and I knew the gun shot was coming next. *The gun shot was coming*! My entire body pulsed, like a beat in a rap song. *Boom. Boom.* What if it was Donny's gun! I had seen his gun.

I had to run! *Now*!

I bolted out of the blocks.

Suddenly there were two shots. Two shots. *Why two*?

I heard someone calling my name, telling me to stop running. And that I had to go back. I turned and looked back at the starting line. Everyone was lining up again. Okay. I would too.

I walked back. I didn't see Donny anywhere. I wasn't shaking as much.

"That's a false start for lane six." Mr. Rossi looked right at me.

"Line up again," said the guy in the lane beside me. Then he looked at me and whispered, "Go when the gun goes, okay? You go early again and you'll be disqualified. They're giving you a second chance."

Disqualified? I didn't know what that meant. But I got low again. And I crouched. And I waited.

I heard Mr. Rossi call out, "Runners. On your marks."

I was in position. What did *disqualified* mean again? I shook my head.

"Set!" Mr. Rossi yelled.

I looked over, saw him lift his hand in the air, and he was holding the gun in his hand.

I had held Donny's gun in my hand.

What if they found my fingerprints?

I had to go. I had to GO.

The gun shot was coming.

I took off.

CHAPTER SIXTEEN
SAM

"**W**as that him again?" Randy asked after the gun went off again for the second time to tell the runners there had been a second false start.

Stuart's family had wanted to stand beside me while Stuart ran. We were all at the finish line, as was the Best Buddies group with all their homemade signs. With a huge grin on her face, Gloria was waving hers in the air like it was a flag on a windy day. Willa had made one on black construction paper with white chalk, and looked like maybe there was a skull on it? Yeah, that was Willa, all right.

I looked at Randy and the rest of Stuart's family and held up my hands. "Stay here. I'll go down," I said.

His mother put her hand on her chest. "Oh, I hope it wasn't him."

"You sure you don't want us there?" His dad had this really loud, low voice. It was one thing to look like a linebacker, but he had the voice to go with his muscles. When I first met him, I was intimidated big time.

I didn't know how to respond to him. This was my fault. Mr. Rossi told me to tell him about the false start, but I didn't do a very good job of it.

"Mr. Williams," I said. "I'm okay to do this."

He gestured briefly with his head toward the start line. "Go."

I hustled down, knowing that, yes, it was Stuart who had false-started twice. *Crap. Crap. Crap.* I hadn't told him about false starts all because he'd been in a bad mood and I was afraid of getting in his head.

When I got to the start line, Stuart was already arguing with Mr. Rossi, telling him he wanted to run.

"It's not fair," he said.

I tried to get a hold of his elbow and remove him, but he jerked his arm away. "I can do this," he said, his voice shaking. "I can."

Mr. Rossi glanced at me and gave me the *I'm so sorry* headshake and the *what can I do?* shrug. Yes, competition was competition and there were rules. I got that. I did. In this situation we had no choice but to accept his disqualification.

What was I thinking? It had been my idea to have Stuart play in the big leagues, unlike Best Buddies where he got to cheat at dodgeball and do whatever he wanted. Half the time I let him cheat, just for fun. And now I'd neglected to tell him a crucial piece of information. I'd set him up for failure.

"Come on, Stuart," I said in as calm a voice as I could, "let's just walk away." All I could think was *walk, walk walk, don't run. Please don't run.*

Stuart turned to look at me and that's when I saw the tears, sliding down the side of his face. My heart felt like it had snapped in two. Seriously. I ached inside. Almost worse than when I physically had heart failure. I'd never seen Stuart cry before, even when kids were mean to him, or when he was in trouble, or when he tripped and fell in the hall from running too fast.

"I want to race," he whimpered.

"You will," I said. "Just not in this race."

"I'm good," he said, looking up at me. The pain in his eyes was real. "I'm fast," he said. "I can do this." His fists were clenched, and I knew they were not clenched because he was going to lose it and take off. They were actually clenched in frustration, and this was how any athlete would feel at being disqualified. Frustrated. Disappointed. And, as a first-time runner, confused.

175

I remembered the first time I fouled out in basketball, before the half was even up. I had to sit and watch the entire game from the bench. I had clenched my fists the entire time.

"I know you're fast," I said to him. "But you were disqualified, Little Man." I looked him right in the eyes. "But you've still got two races left." I held up two fingers. "Two. You are not disqualified from either the 200 or 400 metre races. So, let's walk it out. Forget about that race and move on to your next race."

"But why can't I run *now*?" He tilted his head and looked at the track and the other seven runners lining up again, getting ready to go. "I want to run in lane six. No one is running in lane six now. It's my lane."

"You can run later," I said. I put my hand on the middle of his back and tried to guide him away from the start line. "Just not in this race, okay? Let's talk as we walk."

A few steps later, I put my arm around his shoulder. At least his body didn't feel tensed, like he was going to make a mad dash back toward the start line and get into lane six. In fact, he felt the opposite: limp, like his muscles were mushy.

"You're not the only one to be disqualified in the history of the 100-metre dash," I said, hoping to lighten the situation. "It happens all the time. I bet Andre De Grasse has done it before. They sometimes do it in huge races, like in the World Championships."

He stared at me.

"I bet if we google it we will find out he did. Maybe we should think of something to keep you in the blocks and keep you still until the gun goes off."

He shrugged.

What could I do to help him? Something simple. Something he could remember. Nothing complicated.

I thought and thought as we walked away. In the distance, I heard

Mr. Rossi shoot off the gun to restart the race, and I grabbed hold of Stuart's arm.

He shook me off. "Don't," he said. "I know it's not time to run."

I was almost taken aback by his understanding. Maybe I should try to get to the bottom of what had made him false start. "What made you go before the gun went off?" I asked.

"I dunno."

Maybe not. "Well, whatever it was, let's think about something else."

"Okay," he said.

"Why don't you just stare forward until you hear it. Wait for it instead of trying to go exactly when it's shot." I said to him. "That's simple. We'll practise. And a false start is when you go before the gun goes off and you can't do that."

"I know that *now*," he said.

At this point, I just wanted him to race and feel the accomplishment of finishing. He was fast, so there was the chance that even if he was behind by a little off the start, he could catch up and place, maybe get on to the final. But did that matter? Being in the race and finishing was what was important now. I needed to change *my* focus.

He nodded.

"Let's go somewhere and practise," I said.

As we continued walking, I saw his parents coming toward us, and I waved. "There are your parents," I said.

"They might be mad at me."

"Not a chance," I said. "Look they're smiling." And they were.

When they were close, Stuart said, "I can't run. I went before the gun. Two times."

"That's okay," said his mother. She slung her arm around him. "Lots of people get disqualified when they first start running."

"Even Olympians get disqualified, Stu," boomed his father's voice.

Stuart tilted his head and looked at his father. "Did Donny get shot by the police?"

His father blinked. So did I. Where had *that* come from? I mean, what did Dunn have to do with any of this? Stuart's thought processes always surprised me. I'd assumed that he'd been disqualified because of nerves. But maybe there was something about the gun and Donny that made him jumpy. Stuart sure could be complicated.

His mother gently lifted his chin with her finger. "No," she said. "He didn't shoot anyone and no one shot him. He sold drugs. And don't you be thinking of him now, you hear? You just concentrate on running."

"I checked the schedule and you still have some more races coming up," said his dad.

"And we've got a strategy we are going to practise," I said.

His mother patted his shoulder, followed by his father. "We'll leave you then and go find the others." His mother glanced at me. "Stuart," she said. "Dad wants to talk to you for a second."

Stuart went with his father and his mother said to me, "That Donatello character was arrested last night. Stuart knows about it. Find something else for him to focus on, if you can."

Once he finished talking to his dad, I took Stuart over to a private place by the swing set and had him pretend he was in the blocks.

"Just think about running between the lines," I said. "And nothing else. Stare at the lines and only think about being between them, got it?"

He got into place.

Now it was my turn to act like the race starter.

"On your marks!" I paused for a quick second. "Set!" I paused again. "Bang!" I yelled.

He took off and I called him back.

"That was great," I said. "Good for you."

"So I wasn't *disqualified* that time?" he asked. "That's a big word."

"You were perfect that time! And it is a big word," I said. "You went on BANG and that's exactly what you have to do."

We did it another ten times and then when I thought it had sunk in, I told him we should go back to the track area to get some water and stretch and get ready for his race. As we were walking, we saw the Best Buddies group. Justin and Anna came over to us, still holding their signs.

When Anna saw him she rocked her sign back and forth. "Go, Stuart, go!" she said, grinning.

"You're going to kill the 200," said Justin. He gave him a thumbs-up.

"I was *disqualified*," said Stuart.

"Don't worry about that," said Anna. "You have another race."

"We'll all still wait at the finish line," said Justin. "And we'll be cheering for you."

Stuart nodded.

When it was time for the 200-metre junior boys race, I took Stuart to the start line. Mr. Rossi looked at me and nodded. I listened as he called out the numbers and breathed a sigh of relief when I heard that Stuart was in lane six.

"Lane six, Little Man," I said. *Thank you, Mr. Rossi!*

Stuart nodded and grinned at me. I blew out a rush of air. Time to give this another shot.

"Remember what we practised?" I asked him.

He looked at me for a moment, head tilted and, I swear, my heart dropped right to the end of my big toe. Did he not remember what we practised? I knew he forgot math equations from one day to the next, but this was different. Plus, we had just gone over it.

Then he said, "Stare straight ahead and think about running between the lines. And wait until I hear the gun before I go."

"Yes!" Okay, I needed to calm down, take a breath, and not show him that my heart was pounding too.

Mr. Rossi's voice sounded from the start line. "Junior boys 200 metres, first heat, line up."

"Go, Stuart. Lane six."

I inhaled a deep breath and held it as I watched him walk toward lane six. Once the race started I would get my butt across the field so I could cheer him on at the finish line.

My stomach heaved up and down, like I was the one about to run the race, only worse because I wasn't the one running. It made no sense. My throat felt dry. I had the jitters too. All the nervousness I felt before my own athletic pursuits, I felt now times ten. This was insane. I wanted this so badly for him I could feel it in me, in my body.

My heart beat through my shirt. *Come on, Stuart, you can do this.* I watched as he got to his lane. Saw him look down the track. Was he looking at his lines?

Run straight, Little Man. Just run straight. Simple. I'd made it simple for him.

Mr. Rossi waited as the runners got into place. Then he held up his hand.

"Runners. On your marks," yelled Mr. Rossi. Stuart positioned his feet in his blocks.

"Set!"

Stuart put his hands on the ground and looked forward. I swallowed, my throat parched.

The gun went off.

And so did Stuart. I swear my heart leapt out of my body. He was off! I watched him run, unable to cheer for him, unable to say anything. I felt frozen as I stared at his legs striding forward. He picked up speed, passing two guys on the outside lanes. Then I heard the cheering by the finish line.

I jogged across the field.

"Go, Stuart!" I yelled.

CHAPTER SEVENTEEN
STUART

White lines. I didn't look at the gun. Instead I looked ahead. I had to go around a curve at the beginning of this race. I liked the curves. I waited to be told to get on my marks and get set. Then I heard the gun and bolted out of the blocks, shooting myself forward.

And I ran.

The guy beside me was ahead of me but I knew I could beat him as I went around the curve. I pumped my arms and ran in between my lines. I rounded the first little corner, pretending I was a race car, and caught up to him. I kept going. Moving my legs. Running fast. They felt like they were moving on their own, pushing me forward, and past another guy on my other side. I wanted to do this, run across the finish line.

I rounded the second corner. Then I could hear people cheering for me. I could. They were cheering at the finish line! Now all I had to do was run straight. Straight to the finish line. I passed another guy. And one more. I didn't need to look at the white lines anymore because I could see the finish line.

"Go, Stuart!"

I crossed the finish line and tried to slow down but it was hard because my legs just kept going, like an egg beater. Finally, I was able to start walking. Sam came up behind me and squeezed my shoulder. "You came second!"

"That was fun!" I said, trying to breathe. Holy. My heart was beating a million miles an hour.

Sam held his hand up for a high-five. "You get to race in the finals!" he said.

I high-fived him back. It felt so good to run and race and come second and have someone high-fiving me!

"Later this afternoon is the final," said Sam. "We need to get you stretched and get some water in you and get you some fuel." He gave me a slap on the back, and it was one of those guy kind of slaps, like he gave his basketball players. And his smile was the same, like I was one of them. The same. It made me feel so good inside, like I was full of fizzing soda.

We walked off the track and all the Best Buddies were there with their signs. Justin held up his hand for a high-five and I jumped up and slapped it hard. He laughed.

"Good job," he said.

"That was amazing," said Anna. She held her hands on her chest.

"You zoomed," said Erika, smiling at me. *Zoom. Zoom.*

"Yeeeah," said Madeline. "Goood jooob."

"Yes," said Harrison. "Excellent job. You ran significantly faster in the last 100 metres of the race."

Then suddenly my family was circling me, and they were all smiling and laughing.

"Stuart," said my mother. "You were incredible! I'm so proud of you."

"I'll say," said my dad. "You were crazy fast, kid. I'm impressed."

"He should be," said Declan. "He's been running since he was little."

"You never could catch me," I said to Declan.

"I could so." Declan actually laughed. He wasn't a laughy kind of guy.

"Okay, guys," said my dad. "We should let Stuart get ready for his next race." He pulled a paper from his back pocket. "Looks like you will do the 400 before you do the finals for the 200. Get some grub in you, kid, and some water. Important to stay hydrated."

"I'm hungry," said Declan.

My dad put his hand on my back and said, "We'll go for a bite and come back for your next race."

"Okay," I said.

Sam and I walked back to the track area where all the other kids were sitting, and we sat down with them. He wanted me to stretch but that was boring, so I picked blades of grass and threw them in the air. The grass felt squishy and soft and springy. Suddenly, I jumped up and did a flip because I wanted to because it was squishy. I landed on a lunch.

"Hey!" said the boy who I was beside during the first race. "You just stepped on my lunch."

"Sit down," whispered Sam.

"Okay," I said.

Sam pulled out some money from his pocket and gave it to the kid. I heard him say, "Sorry about that. Go buy some lunch."

"Can I buy lunch too?" I asked. "I want fries."

"Let's go hang out where we were before," said Sam. He stood up and picked up my backpack and we walked over to the same grassy area we were earlier.

"Can I get fries?" I asked again.

"I promise, after you run today." He gave me my backpack. "And you can even order two plates. But right now, eat what your mom packed."

I pulled out my lunch and I had a turkey sandwich, which I liked okay enough. After a few bites I dumped the rest of my lunch on the ground, spilling out an apple, a bag of vegetables, and a stupid fruit-leather strip, but then I found something good. A chocolate power bar. I picked it up and ripped open the wrapper.

As we were sitting and eating lunch, a girl came up to us, and she was wearing jeans and had long, black hair.

"Hey," said Sam. He jumped up right away, like he was a spring.

"Bethany." He almost said this like he was out of breath. I watched the little bump on his throat go up and down.

I stared at him, then I stared at her. They looked like Mary and Owen when they were in the kitchen and going to kiss. I had caught them once, in the kitchen, sucking face.

"Are you guys gonna make out?" I asked.

"Hi, Stuart," said this girl, Bethany.

"How do you know my name?" I asked.

"I met you before at the Best Buddies I Can Play event. Remember, soccer and running?"

Then I did remember. "I ran today and came second. I get to run again."

"That's fabulous. I missed your first run but I'm here to watch the rest." She turned away from me to look back at Sam. "I had a spare last period today, so I thought I'd drop by and watch you guys in action."

"Did you catch the bus over?" he asked her.

"My mother let me borrow her car. I have to pick her up later."

Sam nodded. Then he looked over at me and said, "Stuart, you're going to race in twenty minutes."

Bethany touched Sam's arm and said, "I'll let you guys get focused." Then she smiled at me. "I'll cheer loud," she said.

"I have friends cheering for me," I said. "On the finish line."

"Add me to that list," she said.

"What list?" I asked.

"Your friend list!"

"You're my friend?"

"You betcha," she said, giving me the thumbs-up, just like my other friends do. "I'll be at the finish line, waiting for you to cross."

She walked away from Sam and me, and I watched her black hair swing back and forth.

"Do you like her?" I asked Sam.

"She's my friend."

"Bethany likes me," I said.

"Yeah, Bethany does like you." He patted my back then he glanced at his phone. "But there's no more time to talk about Bethany. You only have twenty minutes, Little Man, before you are racing the 400. Let's practise your start again. Get you refocused."

"Will I use the blocks? That's my favourite part."

Sam smiled. "Yeah, we'll let you use the blocks. Why not? If that's what you want."

Sam made me stretch and do some stupid exercises, but we also practised the start, which I liked, and he reminded me to stare straight ahead and not look at the gun. He told me it was possible Mr. Rossi might not start the next race and I should be ready for that.

"That's okay, I said. "If I don't look at the gun, then I won't even see who is starting the race anyway."

Sam laughed. "Perfect. Don't look at it. Stare straight ahead." Then looked at his watch. "We'd better head over," he said.

We picked up our trash and put it in the trash can. Then we headed over to the starting place.

"You liked how you felt when you finished the last race, right?" Sam asked me as we walked.

"Oh, yeah," I said. And I did like it. It was better than when I shot someone playing a video game.

"Remember that feeling, okay? And go for it again. Just stare straight ahead and go when you hear the gun. And since not as many kids signed up for this race, this is the only one. No heats."

Sam was right, and Mr. Rossi wasn't starting the race, but Mr. Nelson was, and I liked him because he coached the basketball team. He called all us junior boys up to the starting line for the 400-metre race. I had to go once around the track. I could see my family at the start line and all the Best Buddies because we started at the same place we finished. They had signs for me. My name was on them. *My name*. No one had ever made signs for me before. People made them for basketball players, but not for me.

"You're in lane four," said Sam

"Why not six?" I asked. "I like six. I'm always in six." I wanted to be in lane six and I'd never ever gone in another lane when I raced. It was my lucky lane and I wanted to have it.

"They need you in the middle," said Sam.

"Why?"

"Because that's where they put the fastest runners," he said. He put his hands on my shoulders. "Listen to me." He shook me a little to make me look at him. So I did. "Would you rather *not* race and *not* have that great feeling of crossing the finish line? Or would you rather go in lane four and run the race, and feel fantastic again when you finish?" He stopped talking for a second before he said, "Your choice."

I thought about what he said, and I knew the answer. "I will go in lane four. Do they really put the fastest runners there?"

"You bet. Always in the middle lanes."

I lined up in lane four, like Mr. Nelson wanted me to. I shook out my legs like Sam had told me to do.

Then, when Mr. Nelson said, "Runners, on your marks," I got in the blocks.

Then he said, "Set," and I put my hands down. I looked straight ahead and when the gun fired, I bolted forward.

At first it was kind of hard because some kids started faster than me, but on the first turn I caught them. Two boys in the lanes closest to the grass were a bit ahead of me, and I wanted to catch them too.

I kept running. Even though my legs were boiling inside, and my heart was hammering against my shirt, I didn't stop. On the straight part I passed someone else, and it was the guy I didn't like. *Sucker.*

I kept running. Pumping my arms. Stretching my legs. I was over halfway. My legs hurt so much but I could see the next corner. I rounded it and ran around the bend, my legs kind of like propellers going round and round. I heard everyone yelling for me, screaming my name, like I was Andre De Grasse. Suddenly I felt like I was going to explode inside but I was so close to the finish line.

Don't stop. Don't stop. Don't stop.

I knew I was in first because everyone was behind me. I could hear feet, pounding, trying to catch me. I pushed and pushed. Forward. I was close. So close. The cheering got louder and louder.

I crossed the finish line.

I WON! I held my arms in the air like all the runners on television did.

I tried to slow down but it was hard because I was going so fast. And when I did try to stop, my legs felt really wobbly. Like I might fall down. I doubled over and tried to breathe. And stop my legs from shaking so much. People patted my back.

"That was amazing!" I could hear Sam, but I couldn't stand up straight. Not yet. My heart was still going way too fast. Finally, I caught my breath and stood up and Sam hugged me.

"You won!"

"I know," I said. "Everyone was behind me." I think I was smiling pretty big too because my cheeks hurt like crazy. My legs still felt so rubbery, and sweat dripped down my face and off my chin. Sam walked beside me as we headed off the track and onto the grass area.

"I won," I said to my family.

"You sure did," said my dad. He gave me a huge hug too. Everyone was hugging me.

"I knew you could do it," said Randy.

"Will I get a trophy?" I asked. I'd seen the basketball players get trophies.

"You'll get a medal," said Sam. "And you get to race next week against all the other schools."

Suddenly all the Best Buddies came up to me, and Bethany was with them, and they all held up their signs and cheered for me. "Go, Stuart, Go!"

"I did GO," I said.

"You sure did," said Justin. "Incredible!"

"When do I get my medal?" I wanted them to give it to me now!

"When the meet is over," said Sam. "You still have the 200-metre race to run."

"Since I'm getting a medal already do I have to run the next race? I already won."

Sam shrugged and looked at my mother. "What do you think?"

My mother looked at me. "Did you like crossing the finish line?" she asked me.

"Yeah. It was so cool."

"Would you like to run again? If you don't run again, that's okay, but just know when the race is over, it's over. It's your choice. What would you like to do?"

"You might get two medals," said Declan. "I'd run if I were you."

"Yes, but he's not you," said my mother. "And it is Stuart's choice."

"Two medals?" I would like two medals. But that meant I would have to win again. "Do I only get a medal for winning?"

"First, second or third," said Sam. "But it's up to you, Little Man. This 200 is only half of what you just ran so you'll be done quicker. But you decide."

I thought about this. I guess I could run one more race. It had been fun to run and win, and it was shorter so I would be done sooner.

"I'll run," I said.

"Great," said Sam. "Let's go stretch and get ready." He turned to everyone who had gathered around me, and it was a lot of people, like I was a real athlete. "Meet us at the finish line. Right, Little Man?"

"Right," I said. "At the finish line."

I didn't win the 200-metre race, but I came third, which meant I would get a bronze medal. We all gathered in a big crowd in front of some boxes that had been set up on the track. Mr. Rossi had a microphone. Some other kids had helped set up the boxes and they were different sizes. Everybody who won got to stand on the boxes, just like at the Olympics.

As I was standing, waiting for my name to be called and to go stand on my box and get my medal, I was starting to feel like I'd been drinking Red Bull all day long. My body was jittery. I wanted my medal. NOW!

"How much longer?" I asked my mother. There were so many people standing with me. Cecil had won the long jump, so he was waiting to get his medal too.

"Mr. Rossi's going to announce everyone now," she said.

"We're going to start with the junior events," said Mr. Rossi into the microphone.

He went through a bunch of events and I tried to listen, I did, but it seemed to be taking so long. *Hurry. Hurry.* My legs shook.

Then I heard my name.

"Stuart Williams."

"That's me," I said.

"It is," said Sam. "This is your gold medal for the 400."

I ran up front and jumped on the first box I saw. Then someone told me what box to stand on, and it was the middle box, so I jumped down and then up onto a higher box, and waved to everyone. The best part was everyone cheered for me. I waved to my mom and dad, and my mother blew me a kiss. So embarrassing. When I got my medal, I couldn't stop staring at it and touching it. It was big and round.

And the next best part was I got two medals. And they were mine.

CHAPTER EIGHTEEN
SAM

When Stuart's name was called, he was so excited that he bounced up on the bronze-medal podium and had to be directed to the one in the middle. As he lowered his head to get his gold medal placed around his neck, shivers ran through my body.

Beside me his mother had her hands crossed on her chest, until she blew him a kiss and he made a face back at her, which made everyone laugh. His father's laugh boomed over them all.

For me, I hadn't felt this kind of adrenalin rush since my playing days, which were really only a month or so ago but felt like years. Our Little Man had done it. When the students watching cheered for him, he lifted his hands like an Olympian would do. Maybe he could become an actual Olympian if he participated in the Special Olympics.

I snuck my hand into Bethany's, just quickly, long enough to squeeze her fingers but not long enough for anyone to notice.

"This is so great," whispered Bethany. "What an accomplishment. For anyone. Just goes to show you."

Cecil was on my other side, waiting for his medal for long jump in the senior boys' event. He put his fingers to his mouth and whistled, loud and clear. Then he clapped, his big basketball hands making a good hearty sound.

"Great job, Little Man!" he called and whistled again.

When the cheering subsided, Cecil nudged me. "You done good with him."

"He's a natural," I replied. "I didn't do nothing but get him on the track. He ran the race."

"Good on ya," he said. Then he leaned into me and whispered, "Pretty hot stuff beside you. Does she really know stats? I mean, what a combo, dude."

I turned to face him, giving him the slash across the throat.

"Gotcha." He held up two fingers in the peace sign with this huge grin on his face. Then he nudged me again with his shoulder, "I miss ya, bro. Let's hang one night. Go to a movie. Eat popcorn. Talk girls. Watch some sports on the tube."

I'd missed him too. I had. I'd cut myself off from everyone. "Bone up on your stats and maybe."

He laughed. "Seriously. You're on."

"Not Friday though," I said. "I'm taking Stuart to a Special Olympics training session."

"You're kiddin' me. For real?" Cecil slapped my back. "That is so cool."

"Yeah," I said. "Can't you just see him in a Team Canada track suit, strutting his stuff?"

On Friday night, Elma drove Stuart and me to the Special Olympics practice. His mother said she would pick us up because she wanted to watch the end of the practice, but she also wanted to give Stuart a little space. We had decided to not make a huge deal of him going because we didn't want to overwhelm him before his 400-metre race in the City track meet next Thursday.

When he saw the indoor track and so many kids, his eyes bugged out of his head. Of course, when I saw Bethany, in her shorts and Special

Olympics t-shirt, sporting a ponytail instead of a ball cap, my eyes also bugged out of my head. She was so sporty and full of energy. As soon as she saw me she waved and ran over.

"Hey," she said in that low, raspy voice of hers. "So great you guys are here! Hey, Stuart. You're going to rock today."

"Hi," he said.

"You ready to run?"

I watched as Stuart walked away with Bethany, not even looking back at me. I took a seat on the sidelines and watched as they progressed from drill to drill. This time I paid more attention to every drill, thinking of how I could work them into a training session.

Man, they were creative. Instead of doing boring things like high knees, they tossed bean bags under their legs, hopping as they did it, making it way more fun. Then they played with the soccer ball and a tennis ball and even hula hoops, where they jumped from one to the other. Stuart loved the games and didn't say he was bored. Not once. I guess I had a lot to learn.

Stuart's mom showed up with Declan when there was fifteen minutes left. They both stood with me as Stuart went around the track, racing against a few other boys who were also fast. Bethany's Best Buddy had speed too—not as fast as Stuart, but fast. It was good for Stuart to have some competition.

"This is so great for him," said Mrs. Williams. "Thank you."

"No thanks needed," I said.

"Hey, Mom," said Declan. "Look over there. Someone's lifting weights."

I glanced at Declan. "You should give the weight-lifting a whirl," I said.

"I should," he said.

The whistle blew, and all the athletes moved to the middle to surround the coaching staff. After a little de-briefing, Stuart was free to go.

"I liked that," he said to us. He looked at me and grinned. "They do way more fun things than you do."

I laughed. "Yeah, I saw."

"It looked like such fun," said his mother. "Get your stuff and we can get a snack on the way home."

"I'm going to do the weight lifting," said Declan.

Mrs. Williams turned to me and asked, "Do you need a lift home?"

"Um, no, thanks," I said. I should get a ride home, but I wanted to try to spend a little bit more time with Bethany, on the off chance she was free. If she was busy, I'd catch the bus home. Whatever. She was worth the effort.

"I can grab a bus." My words sort of squeaked out. "I'm going to go out with a friend."

"Okay," she said. "Have a good evening, and thanks again. We really appreciate what you're doing."

"It's fun for me too," I said.

I waited for Bethany (yeah, I waited for her) and we walked outside together. The night was clear, the sky still a shade of blue, with the moon hanging like a slim and almost translucent banana on the distant horizon.

"He did great," she said.

"It was fun to watch. I was impressed with the creativity in the warm-up and exercises. Wow. I made him do all the boring stuff. You didn't do that stuff last time I came to watch."

She laughed. "We try to make every session fun and different. But I think we did some of the same things. Maybe you weren't paying attention."

I had been paying attention, but to her, not to what they had been doing.

"Stuart loved it." I paused. "You, um, want to go for a drink somewhere? Coffee? Smoothie?"

Suddenly her eyes lit up. "Ice cream! I know the place."

It was a twenty-minute walk to the ice cream place, but I would have gone if it was an hour's walk.

"What school you going to next year?" I asked as we walked.

"Somewhere local. You?"

"Probably local too. Save some money."

"I hear you," she said. "What are you going to take?"

"Not sure. Business, I think. You?"

"Business."

"You want to follow your mom and open a salon?"

"Not a chance. Just not sure what yet. Not that she hasn't been successful—her place is always packed—but I just want something different. Who knows, maybe I'll be an accountant or go to law school."

"Wow. Good for you. I haven't thought that far ahead. My whole life got turned upside down this spring. A lot changed."

"You'll figure it out. So will I. But in the meantime..." She paused, then she smiled huge. "...I also want to stay local because next year is Special Olympics year." She used her shoulders to dance along with her words. "I want to coach and be a part of the International Games. They're in Italy."

She jumped the crack in the street. Then she turned around to face me and walked backwards. "How exciting would that be?"

I laughed. "Italy would be so ultimately *cool*."

I thought about this for a brief second. "How crazy would it be if Stuart made that team?" I murmured. Just thinking about Stuart in a Team Canada tracksuit made *me* smile.

"He can make it," she said, turning around to skip a few steps beside me. She had this insane energy that I'd never seen in any of the girls I knew.

"He's fast." She gave me a bit of a hip-check. "Get your coaching and we can both try to go. It's a goal to work on. And it would be so much fun. I'd even go as the water girl."

Even though she was bouncing beside me, I wanted to hold her hand. I really did. Not to hold her down but to just touch her and get some of that energy. *Come on, Sam.*

As we walked, the sun lowered and was suddenly gone. A chill settled in the dusk. Before I could take her hand, she started untying the shirt she had around her waist. When I noticed her struggling to find the arm hole I did what my father taught me. Always help a lady. Open doors. Help with their coat. In this case a denim shirt.

So, yeah, I touched her in the process. And, yeah, she felt good.

"Thanks," she said.

"No problem," I said. Then for some stupid, idiotic, moronic reason, I blurted out, "You know I have a heart issue."

She stopped walking, and laughed, while shaking her head. Then she grabbed the front of my jacket, looked up at me and said, "I knew that the first day I met you. And then we talked about it in another conversation. *Why* do you keep bringing it up?" She touched my chest. "You have a heart, I've seen it work, and that's all that counts to me."

She continued to look up at me but now she was finished talking. Her mouth was so close to mine. In an extremely bold move I put my arms around her and I kissed her. Right there on the street. And it was AMAZING!

When we broke apart, she leaned her head on my chest. "I can feel your heart beating," she said.

I inhaled and rested my cheek on her hair. My heart *was* beating. I was still alive.

Man, was I alive.

CHAPTER NINETEEN
STUART

Good thing I wasn't going to jail anymore. I wouldn't have been able to run in the City track meet and win another medal. I ran so fast that I won a silver medal. The best part about running is, well, running the race of course and being with Sam at the track meet (and Bethany) and riding on the bus with all the other kids from school. So now I had a gold, silver and a bronze medal.

After the school meet, my dad had helped me screw some hooks on the wall in my room to hang my medals on. When I got home from the City meet, I put my silver medal on another hook in between my gold and bronze medals.

"They look good there," said my mother. She stood at my door.

"I don't want to punch my walls anymore," I said. "I don't want my medals to fall down."

"I'm glad to hear that," she said. "You ready to go for ice cream? A victory cone."

"Can I have three scoops?"

She smiled. "Of course. Let's go. Dad's waiting in the car."

For my three scoops I got tiger tail, chocolate, and moose tracks. Me and my family (well, not Mary and Lewis) ate our cones outside, sitting on a bench. My mother got a kiddie cone. Seriously. Who eats a kiddie cone when you can have an adult cone?

On the way home in the car, Mary called. Her voice was on speaker phone in the car.

"I'm having pains," she said.

"Real pains?" my mother asked.

"I think so. They feel different."

"How long apart?"

Declan looked over at me. "I bet she's having her baby."

They talked a little longer about stuff I didn't care about then they hung up.

"Well, boys," said my mom, turning around to look at Declan and me, "Mary might be having her baby soon."

My dad sped up and drove a little faster than he normally does. But not as fast as Donny. I'd kinda forgotten about him because of my running. I didn't like thinking about him.

"Like, how soon?" said Declan.

"Hard to say." My father turned the corner toward our house.

In the middle of the night, I had heard my mom talking on the phone. I got up from my bed and went to the kitchen. She motioned for me to stay put, instead of telling me to go back to bed. So I sat down at the kitchen table,and looked at the clock. 3:00 am.

"What time did she go in?" my mother asked whoever was on the other end of the phone.

She nodded, then said, "We'll be right over."

As soon as she stopped talking to whoever was on the phone, my mother said, "Mary's having her baby! Right now. She's at the hospital. They're saying she could go quick."

Within minutes, my mother had woken up my father, and Declan woke up too, wondering what all the commotion was about.

"We should all go to the hospital," said my mom. "Now that we're up. We could wait there to hear the news and see the baby right away."

"I don't like hospitals," I said, kicking the chair across from me. Hospitals were stinky.

"We'll just be in the waiting area," said my mother.

The gross smell hit my nostrils and I wasn't even at the hospital. "I don't like hospitals." I crossed my arms over my chest and frowned.

"Stuart, this is different. Mary's having her baby. No one is sick. This is an exciting time to be at the hospital."

"I'm not going!" My body felt all jittery and I was buzzing, and it was different than before when I ran.

I didn't like being up in the middle of the night. It reminded me of escaping out a window from a foster home and then not being able to get back in and being left outside all night. Freezing and shivering. Then in the morning everyone acted like it was my fault.

My mother held up her hands. "Okay. Let's figure this out."

"I'm not going!"

"Okay, Stuart," she said quietly. "We heard you. We are trying to figure out a solution."

"You go," said my dad to my mother. "Keep in touch and I'll come over when it's time. Maybe it will be calmer here."

"Are you sure?" she asked.

"I can stay home with Stuart," said Declan. "We can stay here together."

My mother and father both looked at me.

"We can," I said.

"We would need you to stay home, not go outside, not run anywhere."

"I already ran today," I said. "I don't want to run anymore. Anyway, I don't get medals for running outside." I yawned.

"That's true," said my mother.

"Let's give it a try," said my dad to my mom. "There's not a whole lot the boys can do at the hospital anyways."

"I'm going back to bed," said Declan.

"Me too," I said.

My mom and dad left, and Declan and I went back to bed, but I couldn't sleep. I rolled one way and the next. I sort of wanted to punch the walls. Then I thought of something else to do. So instead of punching my walls, I got up and went to the kitchen and pulled out all the stuff I used to make bracelets. I had picked up a little baby rattle at the store to put on the bracelet.

I was still working when my mother and father came into the kitchen, both of them yawning. My mom was really smiling though. By now it was getting light out. Wow. I hadn't even noticed.

"Did you stay up all night?" she asked, squinting at me.

I held up the bracelet. "I made this."

"Stuart, it's beautiful." Her smile filled her entire face. "Nathan will love it! You're an uncle!"

"Declan said I couldn't be an uncle. And I'd have to go to jail. Who's Nathan?"

"Well, you're not in jail and you're an uncle! Mary and Lewis named their baby Nathan. If you want to take the bracelet to the baby, we can go later this afternoon to the hospital."

"Maybe," I said. I wondered if I didn't go if I would still get to be an uncle.

After going back to bed and sleeping until noon, I did decide to take the bracelet to the hospital. I'm not sure why I decided but I think it was because I wanted to give the bracelet to the baby, now. Not later. Now.

And my mother explained to me that going to the hospital is like me running. Running can be good or not so good. It's good when I run in races and win medals. But bad (my mom says *not so good*, which just means bad) when I run away from someone when I'm not supposed to.

So, my mom said I could go to the hospital for something good, just like I'd run for a medal. I had gone to see Sam and it was bad but going to see a new baby was good.

We picked up Declan from his job at Best Buy and we drove with my mom and dad. When we got there, I walked in with my dad. He told me I couldn't run in the halls, and he held onto my hand. Like, held it tightly.

"I won't run. Sam told me there's a time to run and a time not to run."

"Smart boy," said my dad. He let go of my hand.

When we got to Mary's room there were all kinds of blue balloons, like there was a party going on. Who would have thought going to the hospital was like going to a party? The baby was in a little bin-like thing beside her bed.

I stared down at Nathan, and I couldn't believe how small he was. Then I sat in a chair and my mother put baby Nathan in my arms. Again, I looked down at him only this time he was close to me.

He had his eyes closed. He had the tiniest hands I'd ever seen, and a tiny nose and mouth too. He yawned and stretched and I laughed. I thought he looked more like Mary than Owen. He had black hair and skin that looked like Mary's and not red hair or white skin like Owen's. But I couldn't see his eyes so I didn't know what colour they were. Maybe they were green like Owen's.

"Was I ever this small?" I asked.

"You were," said my mother.

I still stared at him. I couldn't imagine being *this* little. "Did I learn differently when I was just born? Like this?"

"You did. But you're who you are now, and that's special. Just like this little nugget." She stroked the baby's cheek.

Just then he opened his eyes. Were they green? They were!

"Hi," I said. "I'm your Uncle Stuart."

ACKNOWLEDGEMENTS

I am always so appreciative of those who help me when I'm writing a book. Stuart was created because kind people took the time to talk to me about FASD, read my manuscript in its rough form, and offer advice. Thank you to Stacey Wakabayashi, for all of our back and forth emails, for answering my questions (and there were lots), for reading, and for all the resources you provided to me. Stacey Wakabayashi is a Senior Teacher Consultant for the Provincial Outreach Program for FASD in British Columbia. If you are a teacher reading this book please visit www.fasdoutreach.ca for more information on these beautiful children.

Speaking of teachers…I'd like to thank Michael Rossi and Caitlin Mann for their long conversations about the behaviours of children with FASD, especially with the track meet information; Katja Rossi for introducing me to Mr. Wakabayashi; David Rossi for his insight; and Lois Rossi for always reading my books. Yes, "Mr. Rossi," the track coach in the novel is named after the Rossi boys, including Ector Rossi.

Thank you to Jacqueline Popplestone for our long telephone conversations about being the mother of two girls with FASD. Jacqueline does not let FASD define her girls and is always championing the ABILITY within the word DISABILITY. Jacqueline, you are amazing. The world needs more people like you. And thanks to my fabulous author friend, Janet Gurtler, for introducing me to Jacqueline.

Another fabulous author friend, Debby Waldman, introduced me to Dr. Lori West (Lori J. West, MD, DPhil, FRCPC; Canada Research Chair in Cardiac Transplantation; Director, Canadian National Transplant Research Program; Fellow, Canadian Academy of Health Sciences; Professor of Pediatrics, Surgery, Immunology and Pathology/Lab Medicine; Director, Alberta Transplant Institute University of Alberta). As you can see from the list following her name, she was invaluable with her knowledge about Sam's heart condition. Even with her busy schedule, Lori answered my questions and read the parts about Sam.

Thank you to Elma Begovic for all the Bosnian information and for sharing your story about being in a refugee camp in Germany. I named Sam's sister after you!

As for the many organizations I googled, the books I read, and the lectures I attended, thanks to all the writers, speakers and professionals.

And as always, thank you to Clockwise Press for allowing me to write this series and for being so supportive with each and every book. Christie, you are a brilliant editor. Thank you.

ONE-2-ONE BOOKS
By Lorna Schultz Nicholson

Meet Harrison and Anna:

Harrison, a boy with high-functioning autism, is paired with a Anna, a Type-A aspiring med student. As they both venture outside their particular comfort zones, the two teens find their lives intertwining in unexpected ways.

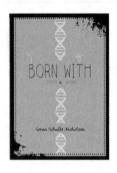

Meet Erika and Gianni:

Erika, born with Down syndrome, is excited to be in the school musical with her Best Buddy, Gianni. Together, they take life-changing steps toward to finding their own versions of success and acceptance.

Meet Madeline and Justin:

An accident left Madeline with a traumatic brain injury; a personal tragedy is tearing Justin's family apart. Can these Best Buddies help each other to reconnect with the important people in their lives—and with the lives they thought they'd lost?